GARGAMEL AND THE SMURFS

Peyo

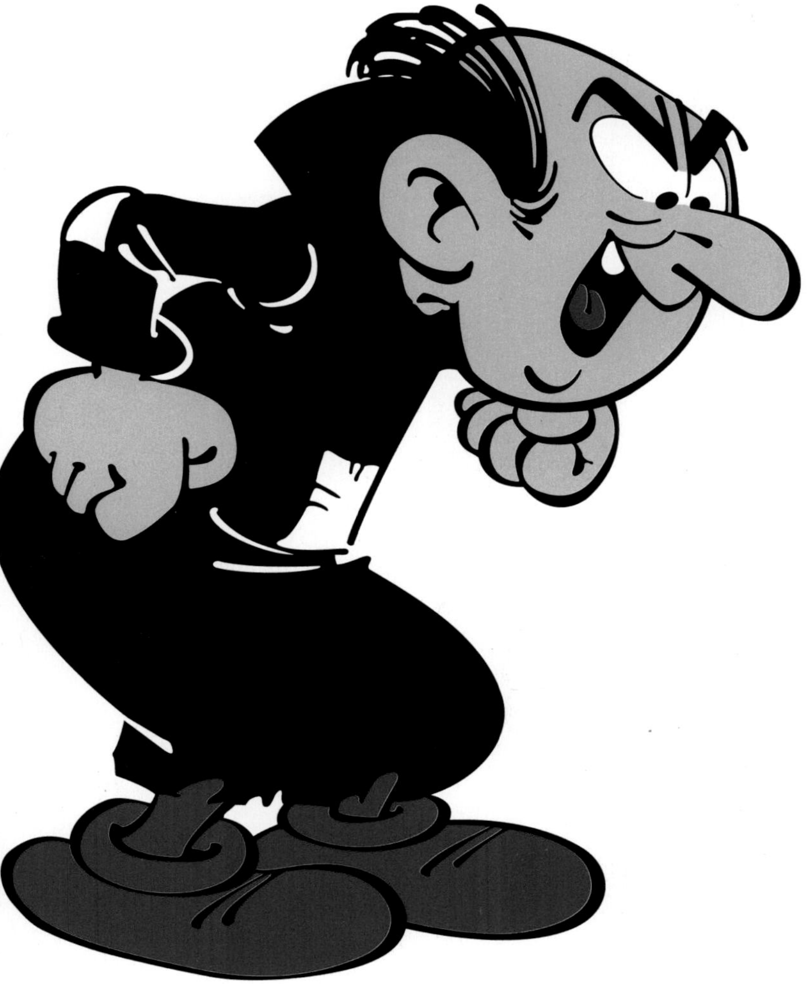

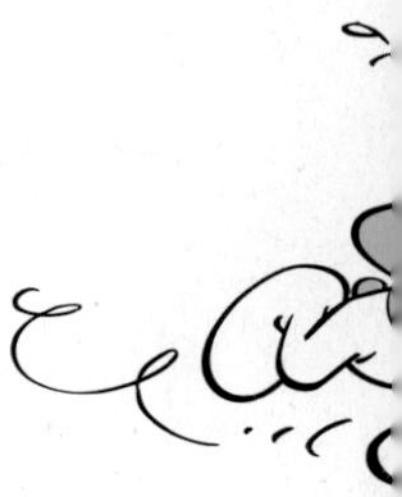

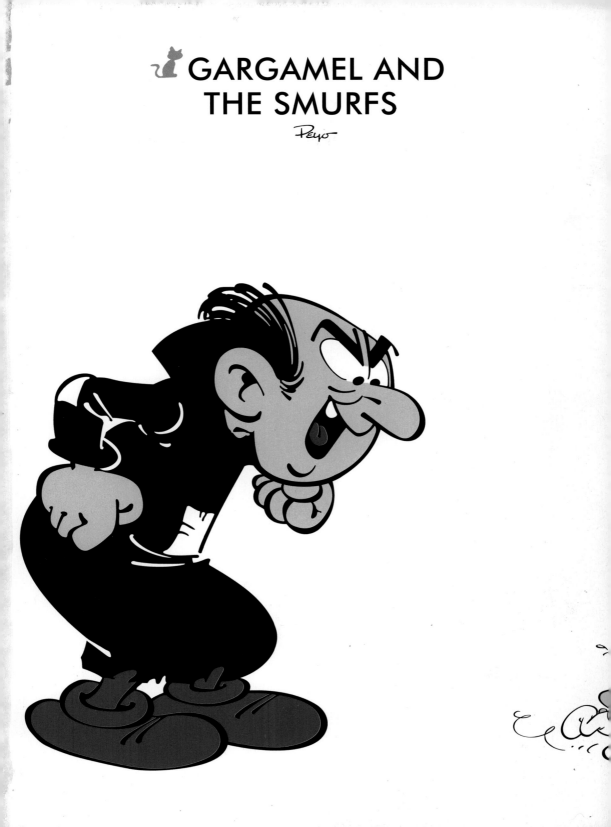

GARGAMEL AND THE SMURFS

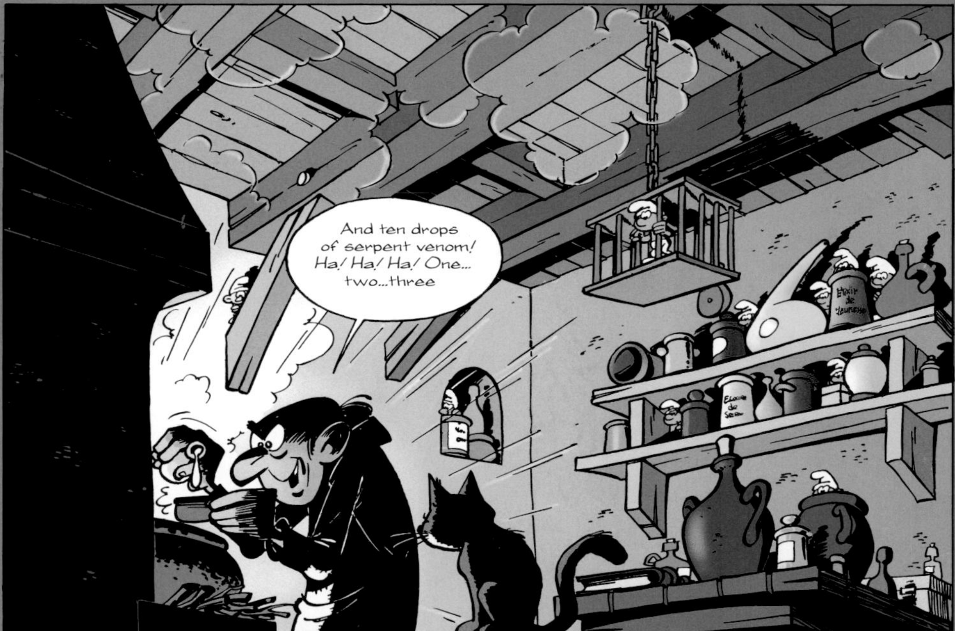
And ten drops of serpent venom! Ha! Ha! Ha! One... two...three

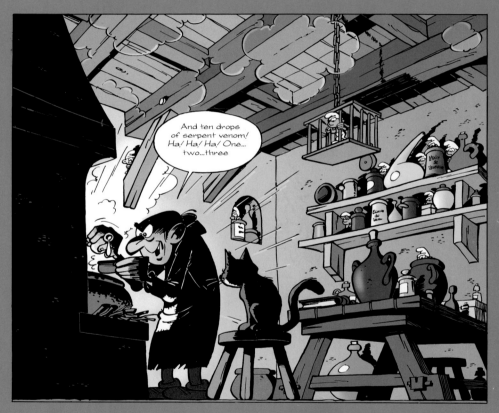

A SMURFS GRAPHIC NOVEL BY Peyo

PAPERCUTZ™
NEW YORK

SMURFS GRAPHIC NOVELS AVAILABLE FROM PAPERCUTZ™

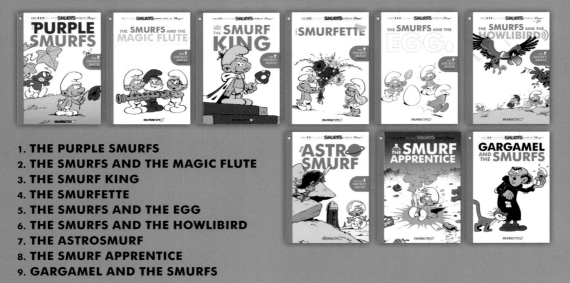

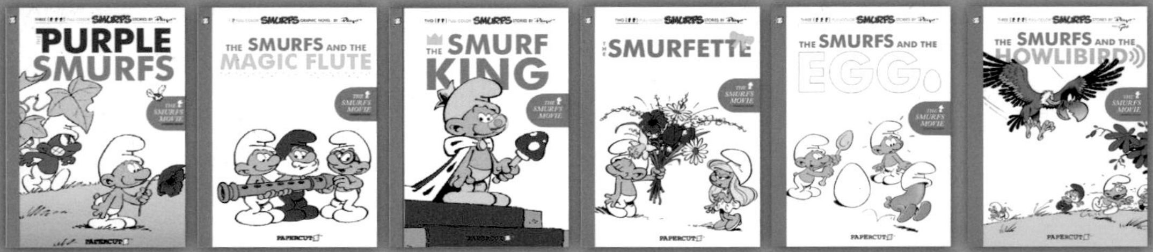
PURPLE SMURFS
THE SMURFS AND THE MAGIC FLUTE
THE SMURF KING
THE SMURFETTE
THE SMURFS AND THE EGG
THE SMURFS AND THE HOWLIBIRD

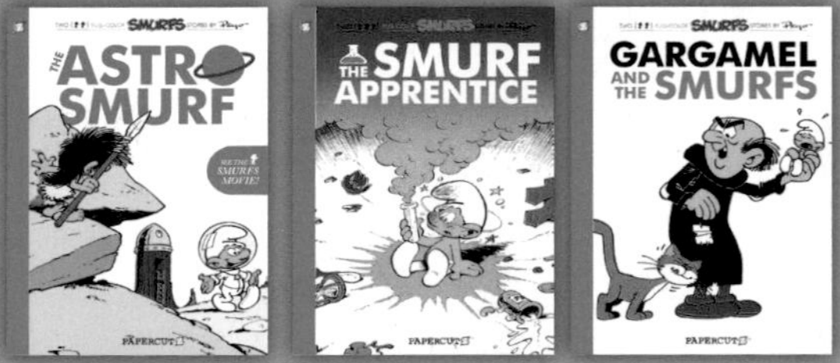
THE ASTRO SMURF
THE SMURF APPRENTICE
GARGAMEL AND THE SMURFS

1. **THE PURPLE SMURFS**
2. **THE SMURFS AND THE MAGIC FLUTE**
3. **THE SMURF KING**
4. **THE SMURFETTE**
5. **THE SMURFS AND THE EGG**
6. **THE SMURFS AND THE HOWLIBIRD**
7. **THE ASTROSMURF**
8. **THE SMURF APPRENTICE**
9. **GARGAMEL AND THE SMURFS**

COMING SOON:

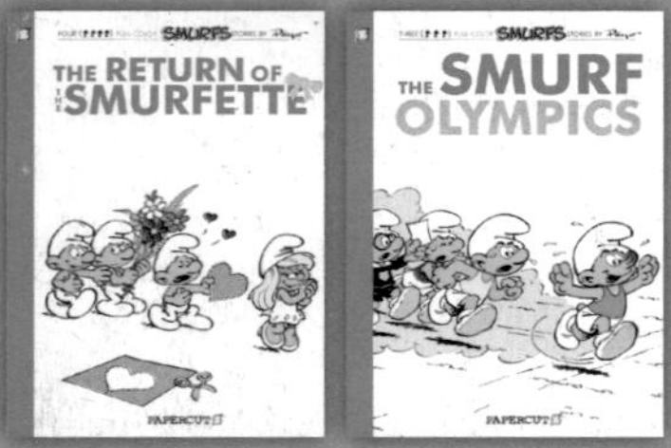
THE RETURN OF THE SMURFETTE
THE SMURF OLYMPICS

10. **THE RETURN OF THE SMURFETTE**
11. **THE SMURF OLYMPICS**

The Smurfs graphic novels are available in paperback for $5.99 each and in hardcover for $10.99 each at booksellers everywhere.

Or order from us. Please add $4.00 for postage and handling for the first book, add $1.00 for each additional book. Please make check payable to NBM Publishing. Send to: PAPERCUTZ, 40 Exchange Place, Ste. 1308, New York, NY 10005 (1-800-886-1223).

WWW.PAPERCUTZ.COM

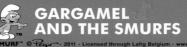

GARGAMEL AND THE SMURFS

"The Smurfnapper"
BY YVAN DELPORTE AND PEYO

"A Smurf Not Like the Others"
BY PEYO

"The Smurfs and the Little Ghost"
BY PEYO

"Sagratamabarb"
BY PEYO

Joe Johnson, *SMURFLATIONS*
Adam Grano, *SMURFIC DESIGN*
Janice Chiang, *LETTERING SMURFETTE*
Matt. Murray, *SMURF CONSULTANT*
Michael Petranek, *ASSOCIATE SMURF*
Jim Salicrup, *SMURF-IN-CHIEF*

PAPERBACK EDITION ISBN: 978-1-59707-289-2
HARDCOVER EDITION ISBN: 978-1-59707-290-8

PRINTED IN CHINA NOVEMBER 2011 BY WKT CO. LTD.
3/F PHASE I LEADER INDUSTRIAL CENTRE
188 TEXACO ROAD, TSEUN WAN, N.T., HONG KONG

DISTRIBUTED BY MACMILLAN
FIRST PAPERCUTZ PRINTING

THE SMURFNAPPER

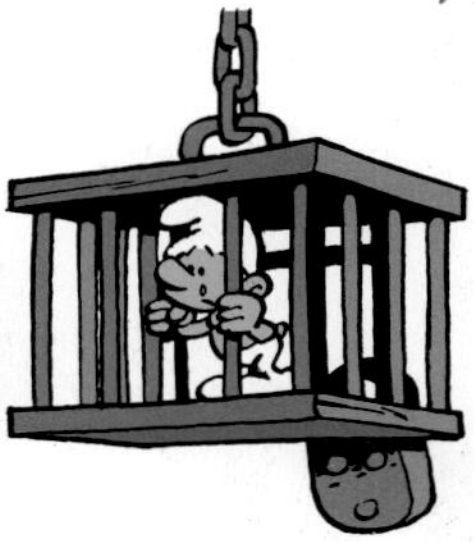

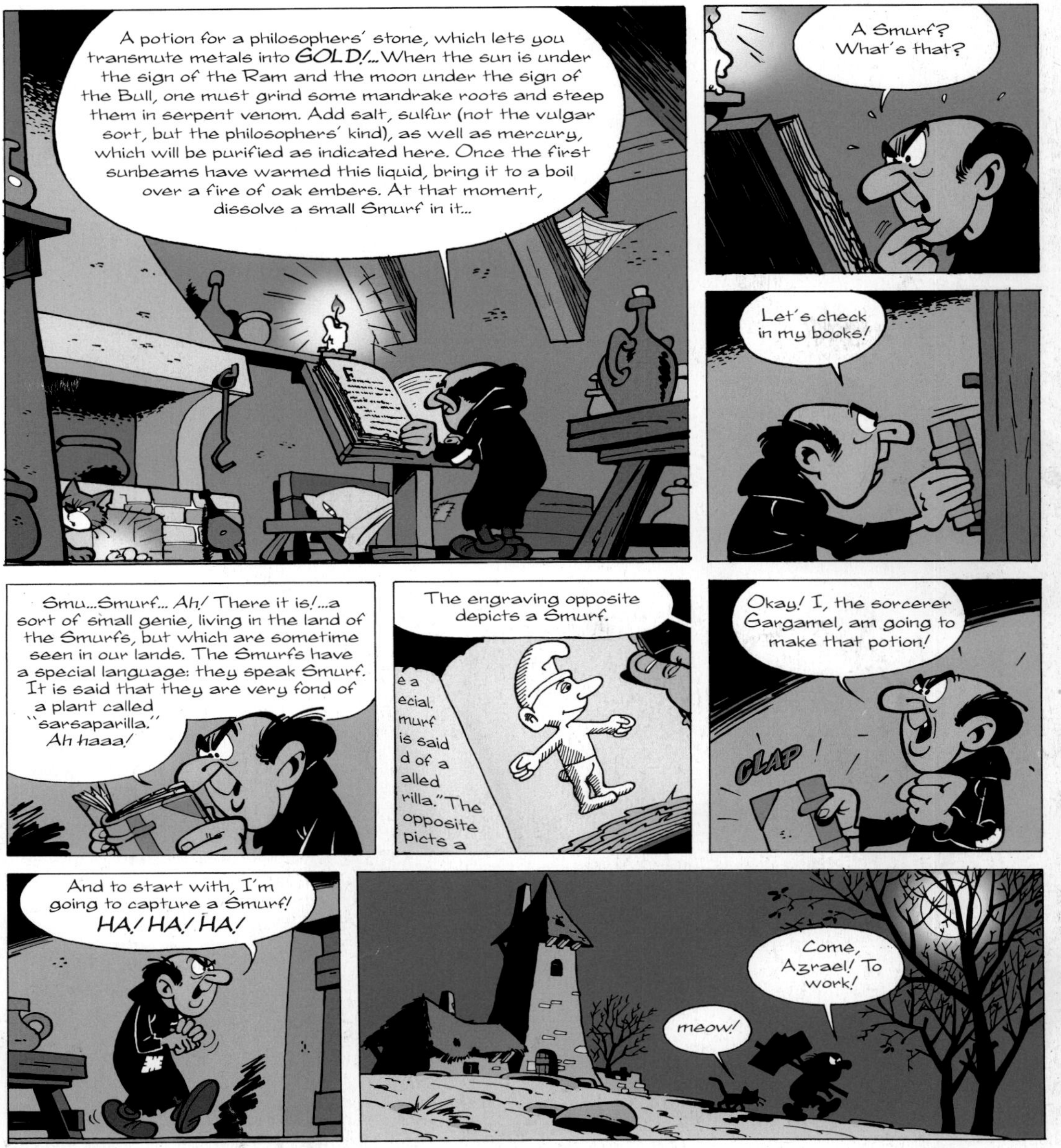

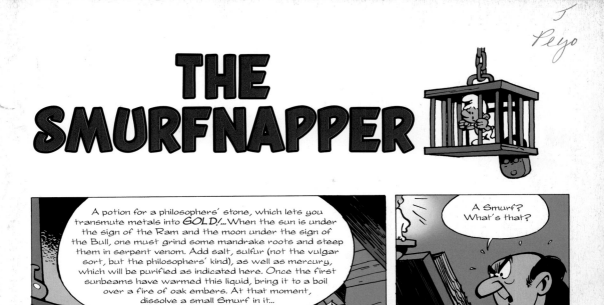

A potion for a philosophers' stone, which lets you transmute metals into GOLD!... When the sun is under the sign of the Ram and the moon under the sign of the Bull, one must grind some mandrake roots and steep them in serpent venom. Add salt, sulfur (not the vulgar sort, but the philosophers' kind), as well as mercury, which will be purified as indicated here. Once the first sunbeams have warmed this liquid, bring it to a boil over a fire of oak embers. At that moment, dissolve a small Smurf in it...
A Smurf? What's that?
Let's check in my books!
Smu...Smurf... Ah! There it is!...a sort of small genie, living in the land of the Smurfs, but which are sometime seen in our lands. The Smurfs have a special language: they speak Smurf. It is said that they are very fond of a plant called "sarsaparilla." Ah haaa!
The engraving opposite depicts a Smurf.
e a
ecial.
murf
is said
d of a
alled
rilla." The
opposite
picts a
Okay! I, the sorcerer Gargamel, am going to make that potion!
CLAP
And to start with, I'm going to capture a Smurf! HA! HA! HA!
Come, Azrael! To work!
meow!

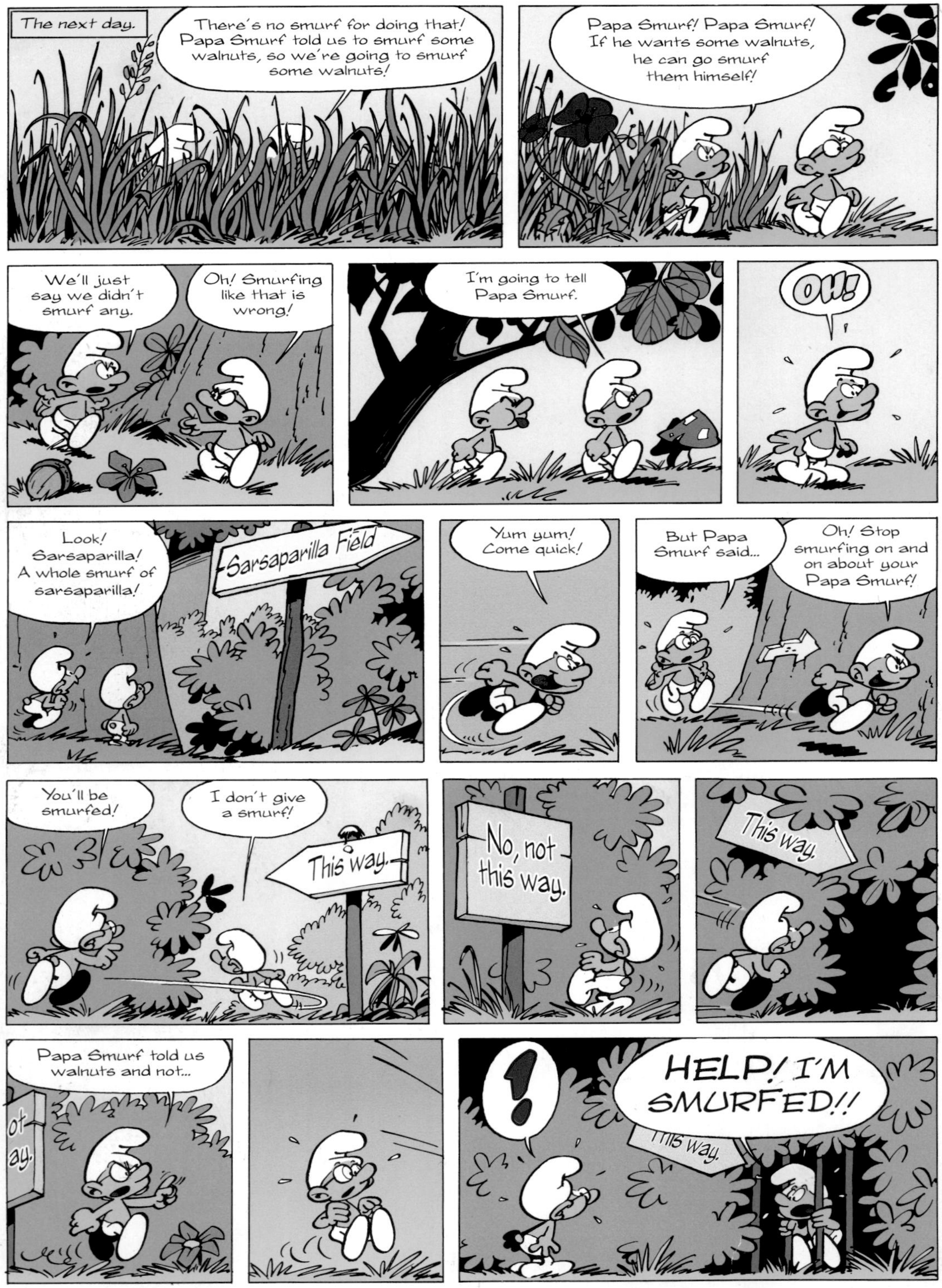

The next day.
There's no smurf for doing that! Papa Smurf told us to smurf some walnuts, so we're going to smurf some walnuts!
Papa Smurf! Papa Smurf! If he wants some walnuts, he can go smurf them himself!
We'll just say we didn't smurf any.
Oh! Smurfing like that is wrong!
I'm going to tell Papa Smurf.
OH!
Look! Sarsaparilla! A whole smurf of sarsaparilla!
Sarsaparilla Field
Yum yum! Come quick!
But Papa Smurf said...
Oh! Stop smurfing on and on about your Papa Smurf!
You'll be smurfed!
I don't give a smurf!
This way.
No, not this way.
This way.
Papa Smurf told us walnuts and not...
!
HELP! I'M SMURFED!!
This way.

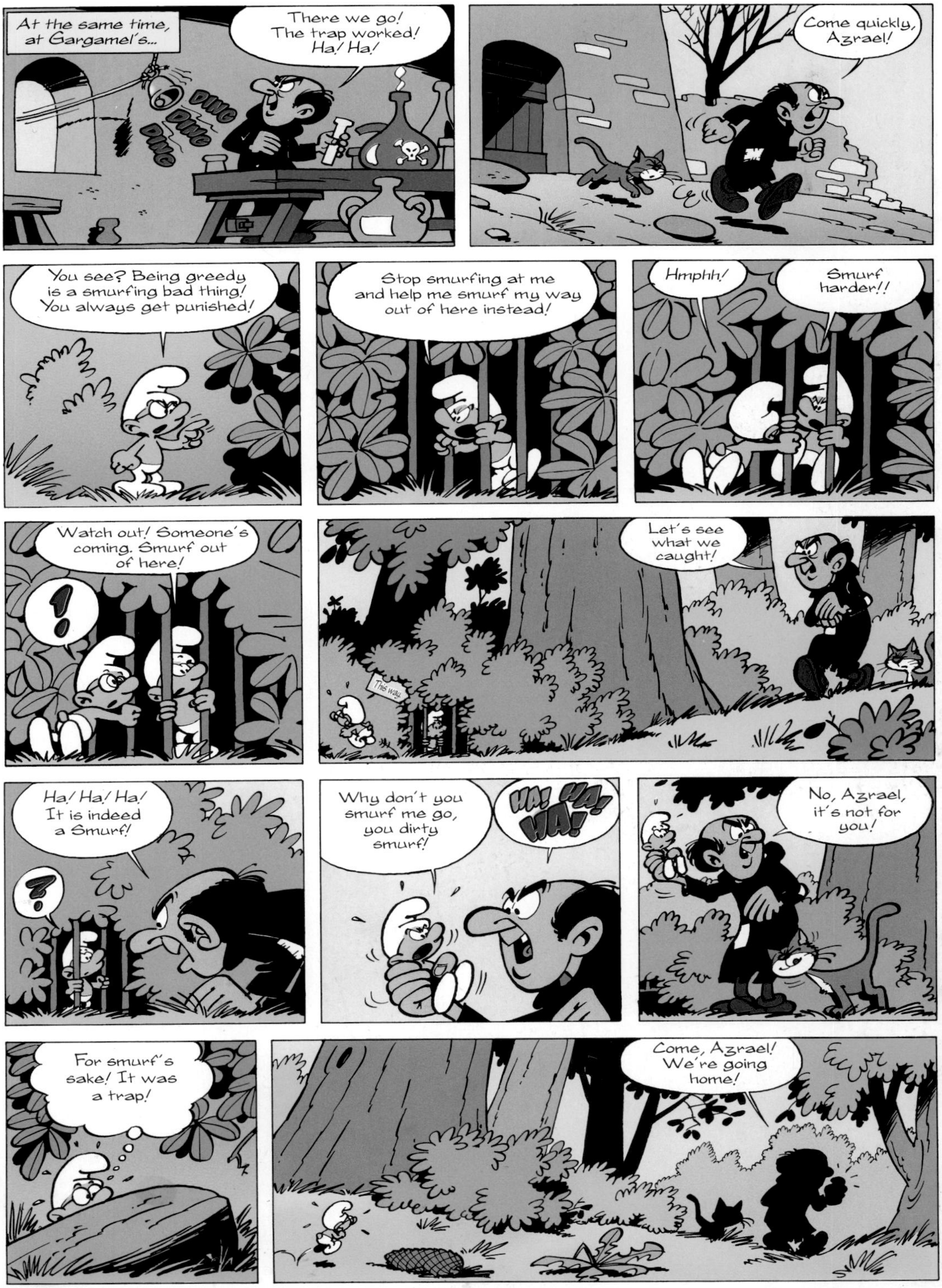

At the same time, at Gargamel's...
There we go! The trap worked! Ha! Ha!
DING DING DING
Come quickly, Azrael!
You see? Being greedy is a smurfing bad thing! You always get punished!
Stop smurfing at me and help me smurf my way out of here instead!
Hmphh!
Smurf harder!!
Watch out! Someone's coming. Smurf out of here!
!
Let's see what we caught!
This way
Ha! Ha! Ha! It is indeed a Smurf!
?
Why don't you smurf me go, you dirty smurf!
HA! HA! HA!
No, Azrael, it's not for you!
For smurf's sake! It was a trap!
Come, Azrael! We're going home!

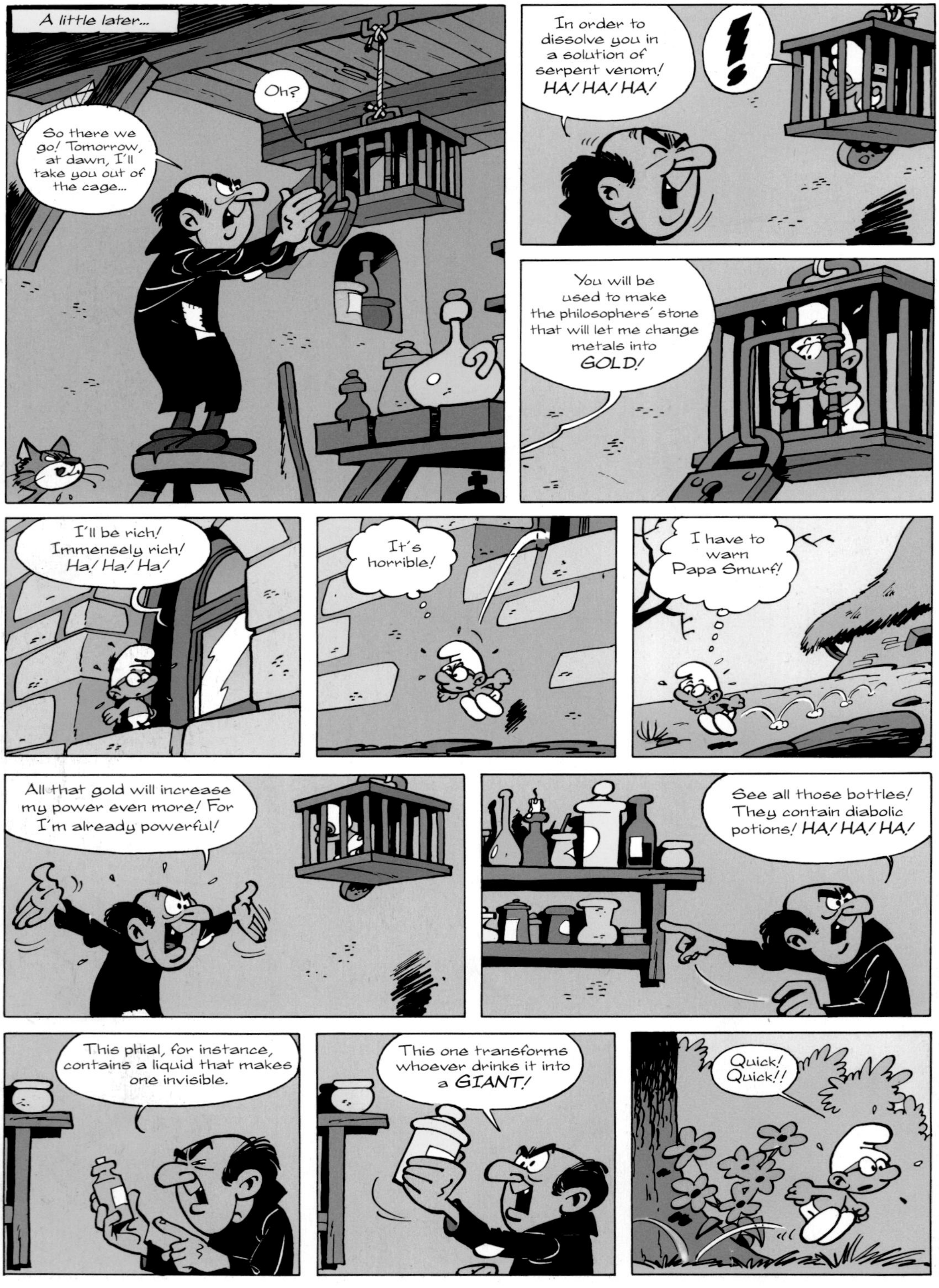

A little later...
So there we go! Tomorrow, at dawn, I'll take you out of the cage...
Oh?
In order to dissolve you in a solution of serpent venom! HA! HA! HA!
You will be used to make the philosophers' stone that will let me change metals into GOLD!
I'll be rich! Immensely rich! Ha! Ha! Ha!
It's horrible!
I have to warn Papa Smurf!
All that gold will increase my power even more! For I'm already powerful!
See all those bottles! They contain diabolic potions! HA! HA! HA!
This phial, for instance, contains a liquid that makes one invisible.
This one transforms whoever drinks it into a GIANT!
Quick! Quick!!

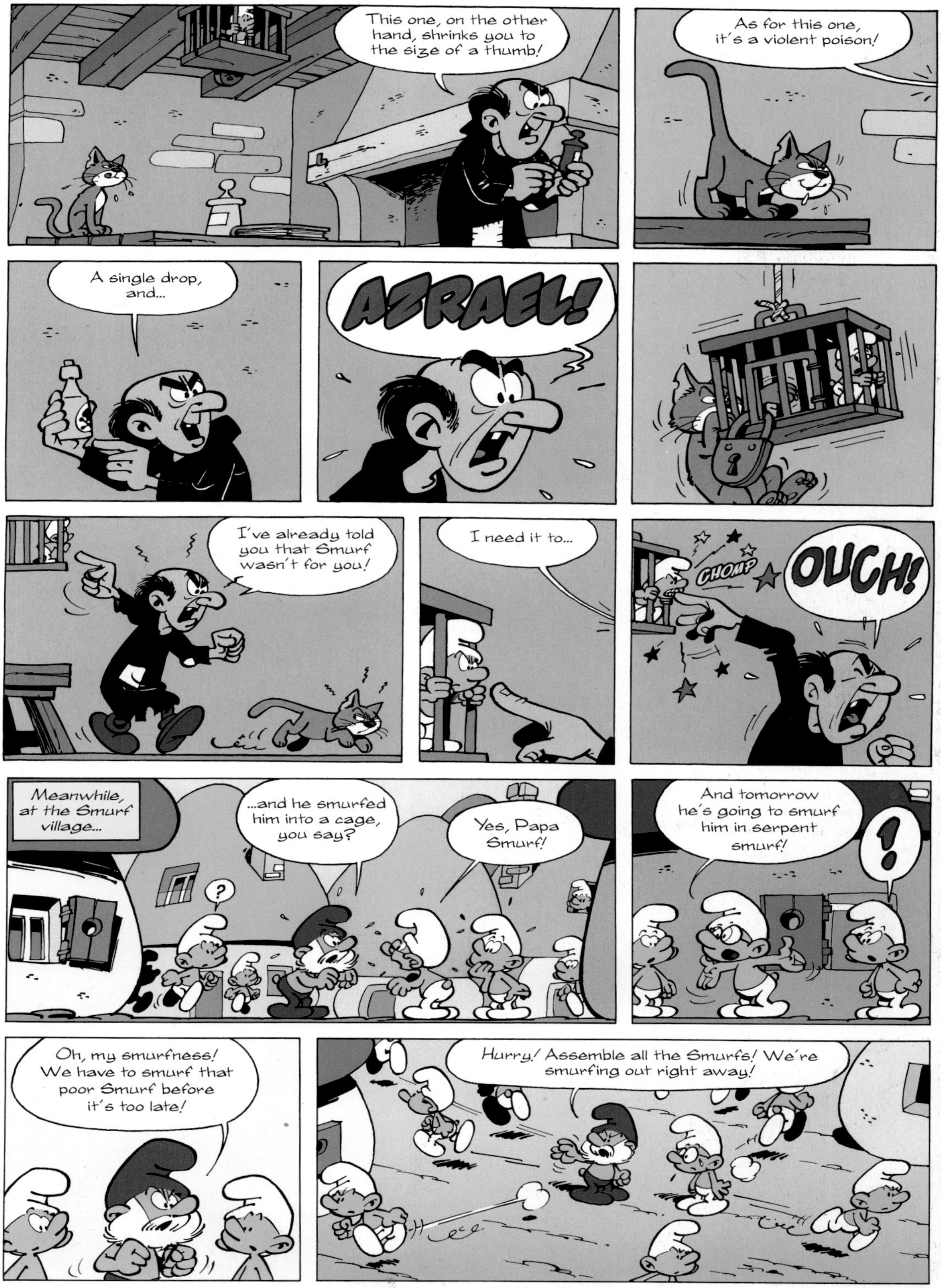

This one, on the other hand, shrinks you to the size of a thumb!
As for this one, it's a violent poison!
A single drop, and...
AZRAEL!
I've already told you that Smurf wasn't for you!
I need it to...
CHOMP
OUCH!
Meanwhile, at the Smurf village...
...and he smurfed him into a cage, you say?
Yes, Papa Smurf!
?
And tomorrow he's going to smurf him in serpent smurf!
!
Oh, my smurfness! We have to smurf that poor Smurf before it's too late!
Hurry! Assemble all the Smurfs! We're smurfing out right away!

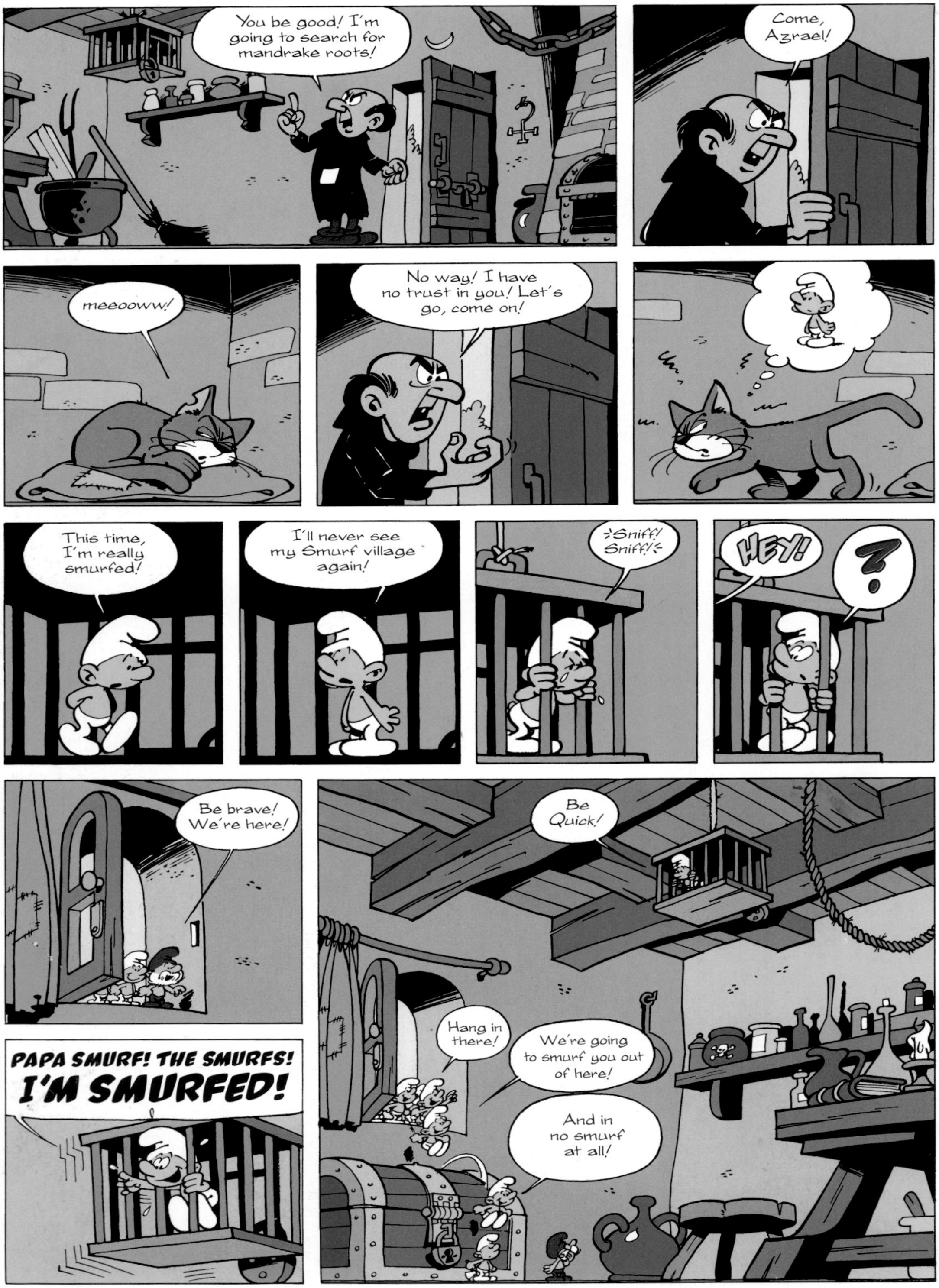
You be good! I'm going to search for mandrake roots!
Come, Azrael!
meeooww!
No way! I have no trust in you! Let's go, come on!
This time, I'm really smurfed!
I'll never see my Smurf village again!
Sniff! Sniff!
HEY!
?
Be brave! We're here!
PAPA SMURF! THE SMURFS! I'M SMURFED!
Be Quick!
Hang in there!
We're going to smurf you out of here!
And in no smurf at all!

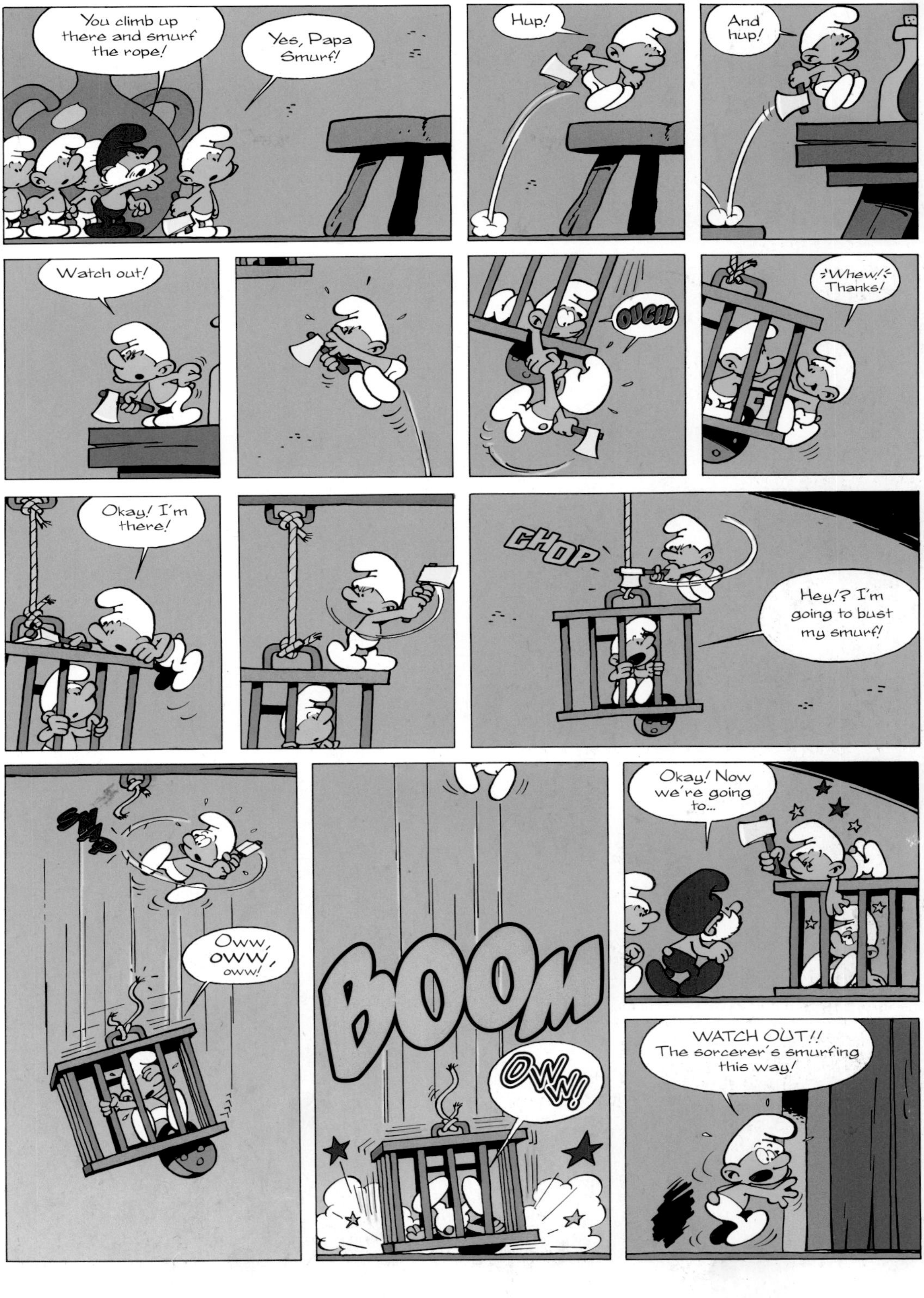
You climb up there and smurf the rope!
Yes, Papa Smurf!
Hup!
And hup!
Watch out!
OUCH!!
Whew! Thanks!
Okay! I'm there!
CHOP
Hey!? I'm going to bust my smurf!
Oww, OWW, oww!
BOOM
OWW!
Okay! Now we're going to...
WATCH OUT!! The sorcerer's smurfing this way!

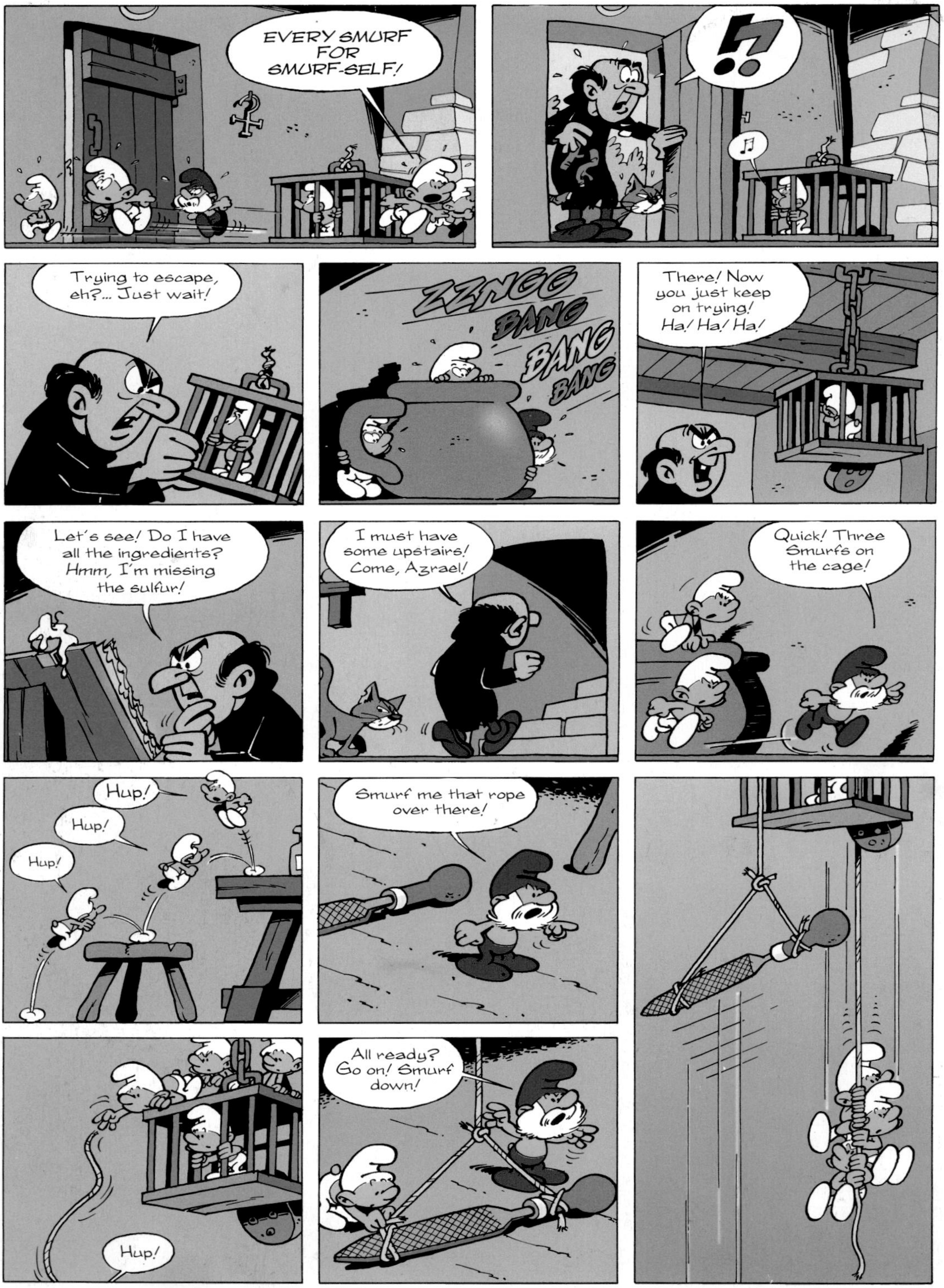
EVERY SMURF FOR SMURF-SELF!
Trying to escape, eh?... Just wait!
ZZNGG
BANG
BANG
BANG
There! Now you just keep on trying! Ha! Ha! Ha!
Let's see! Do I have all the ingredients? Hmm, I'm missing the sulfur!
I must have some upstairs! Come, Azrael!
Quick! Three Smurfs on the cage!
Hup!
Hup!
Hup!
Smurf me that rope over there!
Hup!
All ready? Go on! Smurf down!

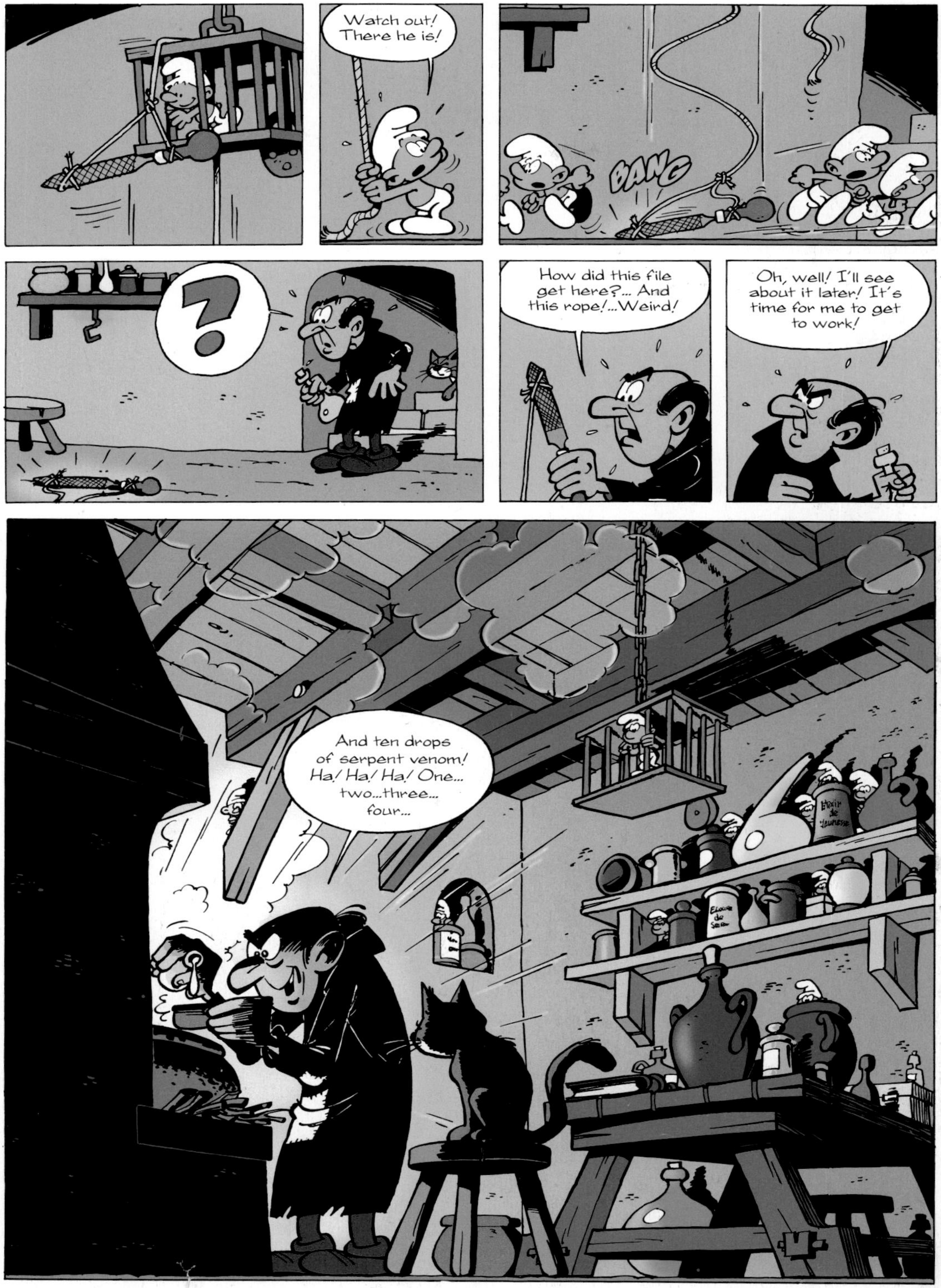

Watch out! There he is!
BANG
How did this file get here?... And this rope!...Weird!
Oh, well! I'll see about it later! It's time for me to get to work!
And ten drops of serpent venom! Ha! Ha! Ha! One... two...three... four...

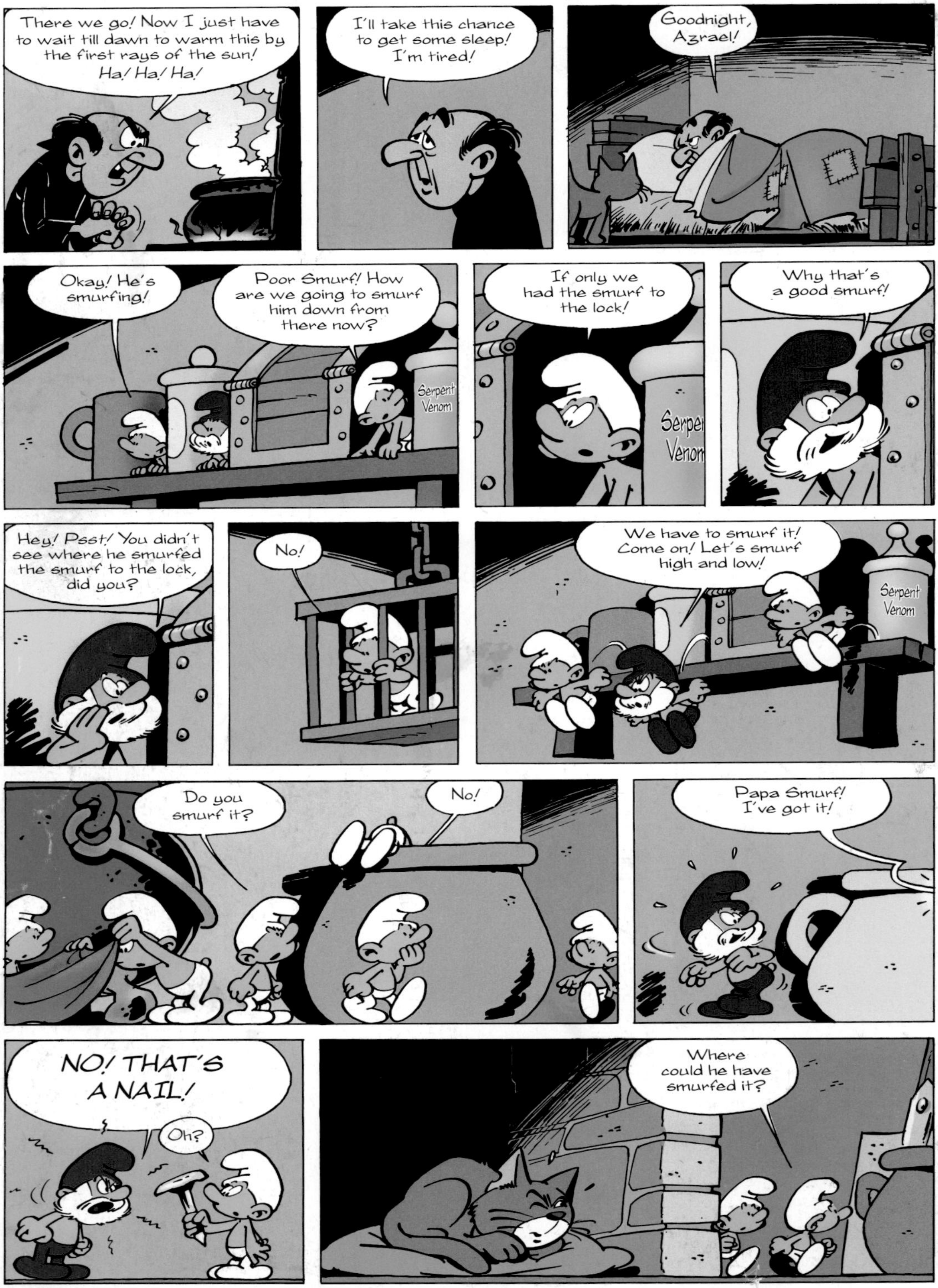
There we go! Now I just have to wait till dawn to warm this by the first rays of the sun! Ha! Ha! Ha!
I'll take this chance to get some sleep! I'm tired!
Goodnight, Azrael!
Okay! He's smurfing!
Poor Smurf! How are we going to smurf him down from there now?
Serpent Venom
If only we had the smurf to the lock!
Serpent Venom
Why that's a good smurf!
Hey! Psst! You didn't see where he smurfed the smurf to the lock, did you?
No!
We have to smurf it! Come on! Let's smurf high and low!
Serpent Venom
Do you smurf it?
No!
Papa Smurf! I've got it!
NO! THAT'S A NAIL!
Oh?
Where could he have smurfed it?

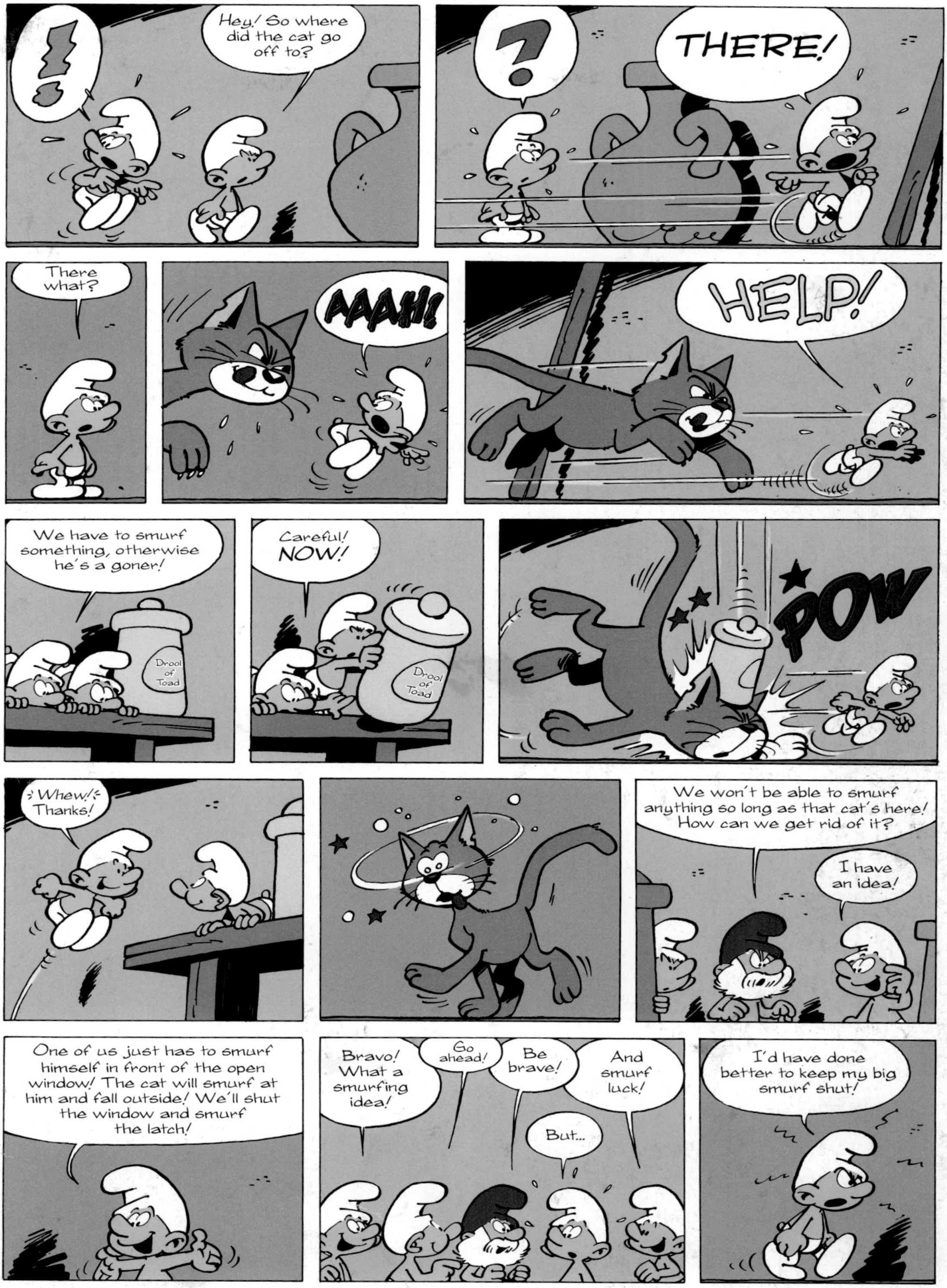
!
Hey! So where did the cat go off to?
?
THERE!
There what?
AAAH!
HELP!
We have to smurf something, otherwise he's a goner!
Drool of Toad
Careful! NOW!
Drool of Toad
POW
Whew! Thanks!
We won't be able to smurf anything so long as that cat's here! How can we get rid of it?
I have an idea!
One of us just has to smurf himself in front of the open window! The cat will smurf at him and fall outside! We'll shut the window and smurf the latch!
Bravo! What a smurfing idea!
Go ahead!
Be brave!
And smurf luck!
But...
I'd have done better to keep my big smurf shut!

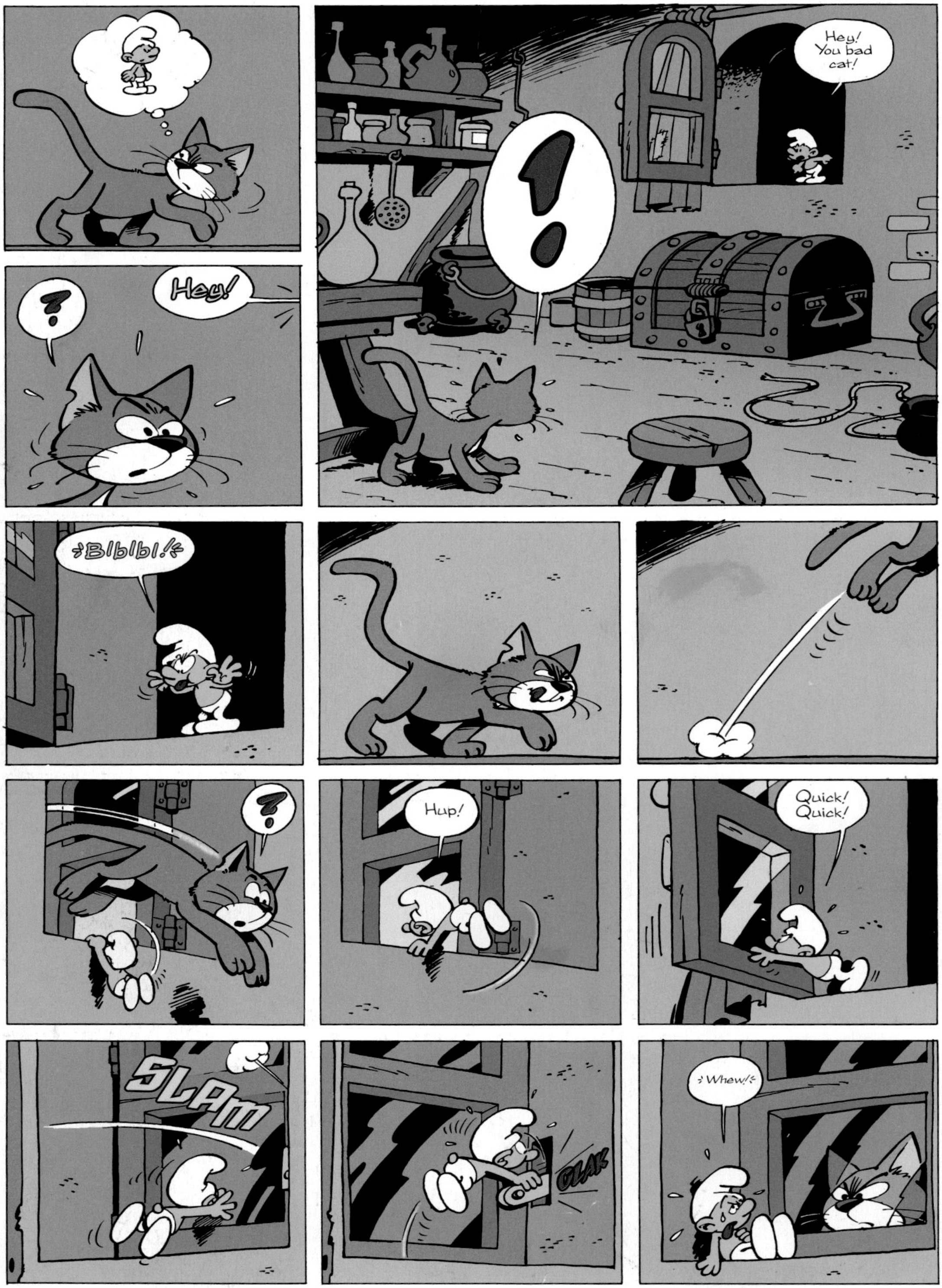
Hey!
?
!
Hey! You bad cat!
Blblbl!
?
Hup!
Quick! Quick!
SLAM
CLAK
Whew!

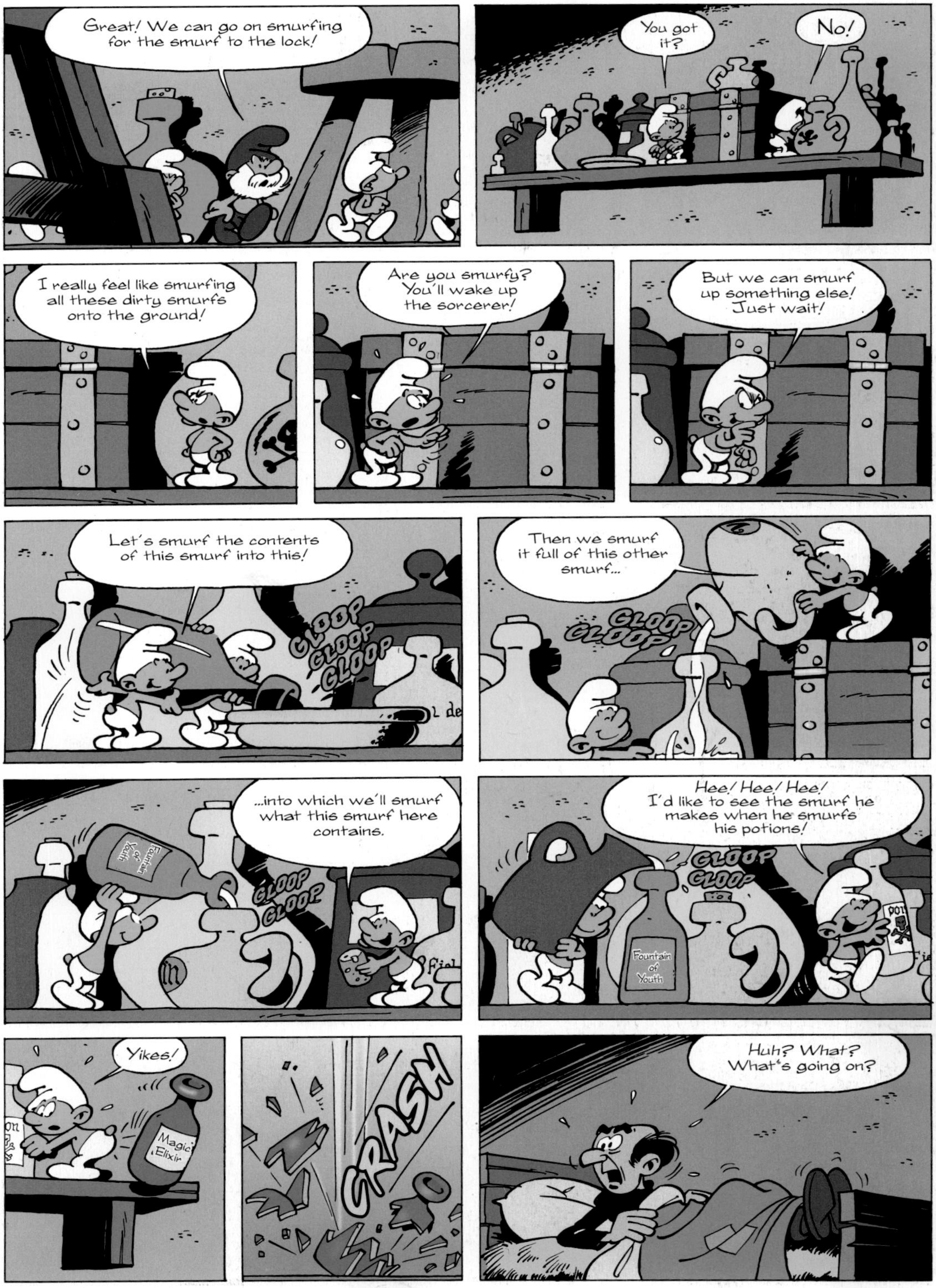

Great! We can go on smurfing for the smurf to the lock!
You got it?
No!
I really feel like smurfing all these dirty smurfs onto the ground!
Are you smurfy? You'll wake up the sorcerer!
But we can smurf up something else! Just wait!
Let's smurf the contents of this smurf into this!
GLOOP GLOOP GLOOP
Then we smurf it full of this other smurf...
GLOOP GLOOP
...into which we'll smurf what this smurf here contains.
Fountain of Youth
GLOOP GLOOP
Hee! Hee! Hee! I'd like to see the smurf he makes when he smurfs his potions!
GLOOP GLOOP
Fountain of Youth
Yikes!
Magic Elixir
CRASH
Huh? What? What's going on?

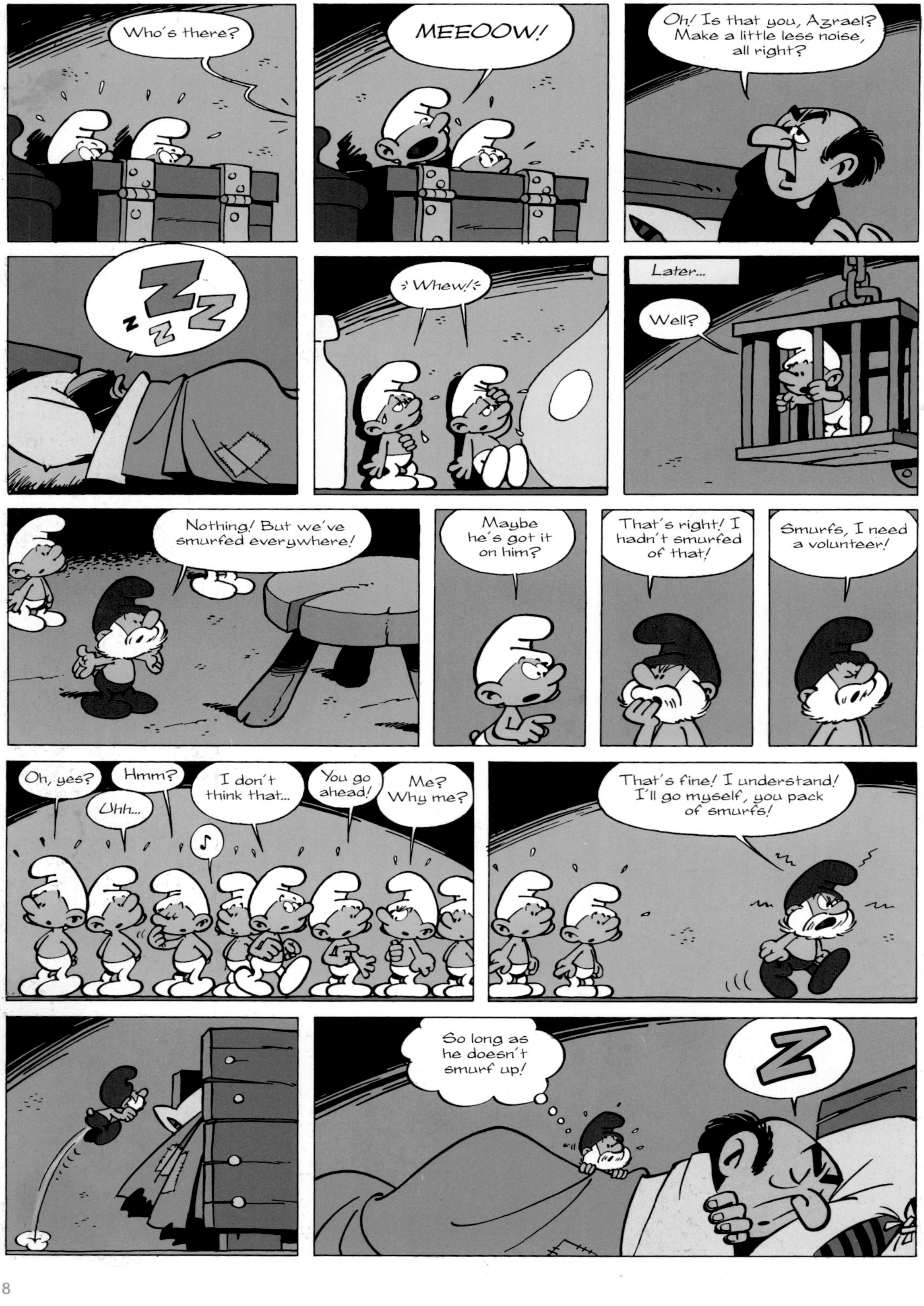

Who's there?
MEEOOW!
Oh! Is that you, Azrael? Make a little less noise, all right?
Z Z Z Z
Whew!
Later...
Well?
Nothing! But we've smurfed everywhere!
Maybe he's got it on him?
That's right! I hadn't smurfed of that!
Smurfs, I need a volunteer!
Oh, yes?
Hmm?
Uhh...
I don't think that...
You go ahead!
Me? Why me?
That's fine! I understand! I'll go myself, you pack of smurfs!
So long as he doesn't smurf up!
Z

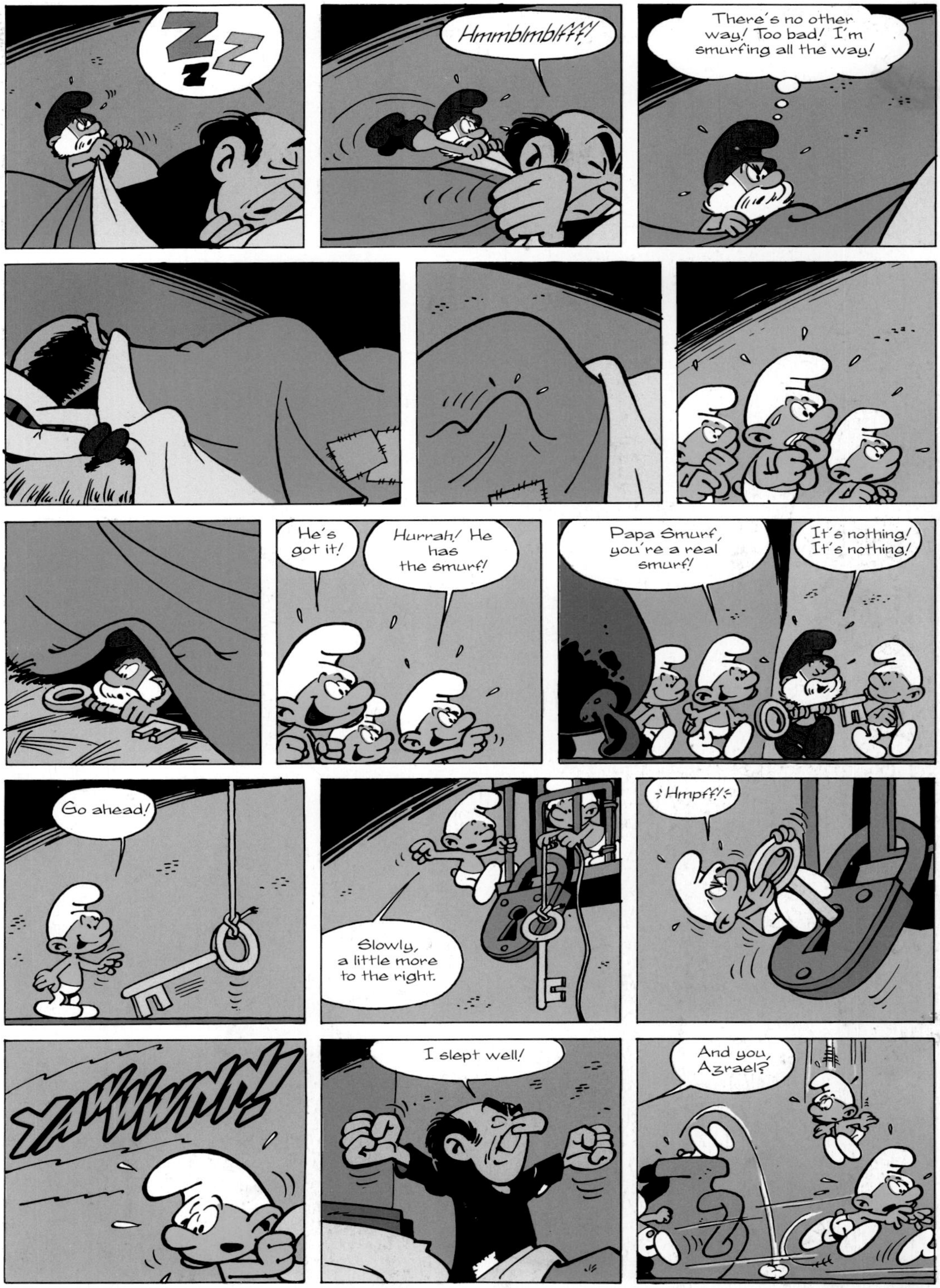
Hmmblmblfff!
There's no other way! Too bad! I'm smurfing all the way!
He's got it!
Hurrah! He has the smurf!
Papa Smurf, you're a real smurf!
It's nothing! It's nothing!
Go ahead!
Slowly, a little more to the right.
Hmpff!
YAWWWNN!
I slept well!
And you, Azrael?

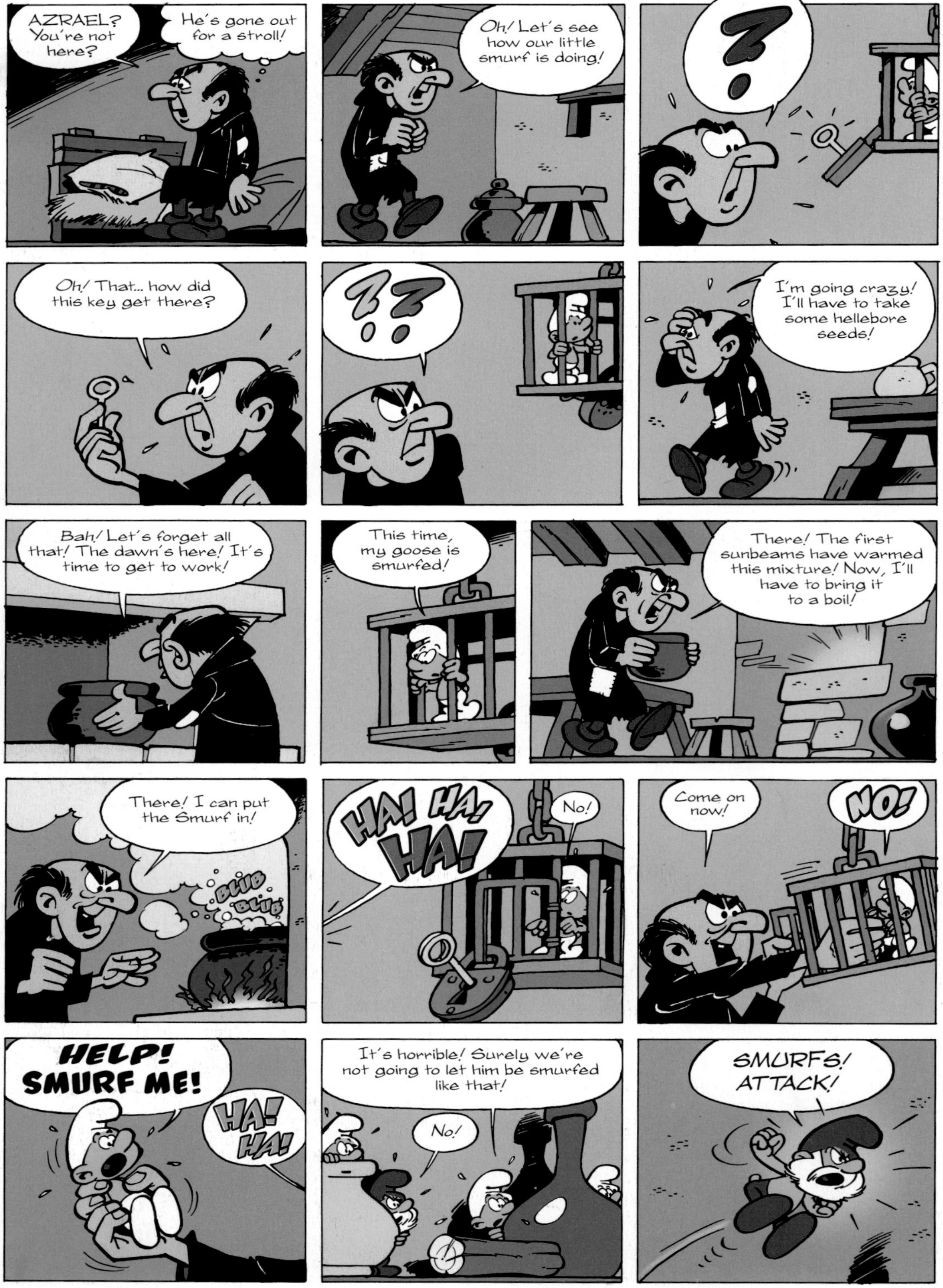
AZRAEL? You're not here?
He's gone out for a stroll!
Oh! Let's see how our little smurf is doing!
?
Oh! That... how did this key get there?
? ?
I'm going crazy! I'll have to take some hellebore seeds!
Bah! Let's forget all that! The dawn's here! It's time to get to work!
This time, my goose is smurfed!
There! The first sunbeams have warmed this mixture! Now, I'll have to bring it to a boil!
There! I can put the Smurf in!
BLUB BLUB
HA! HA! HA!
No!
Come on now!
NO!
HELP! SMURF ME!
HA! HA!
It's horrible! Surely we're not going to let him be smurfed like that!
No!
SMURFS! ATTACK!

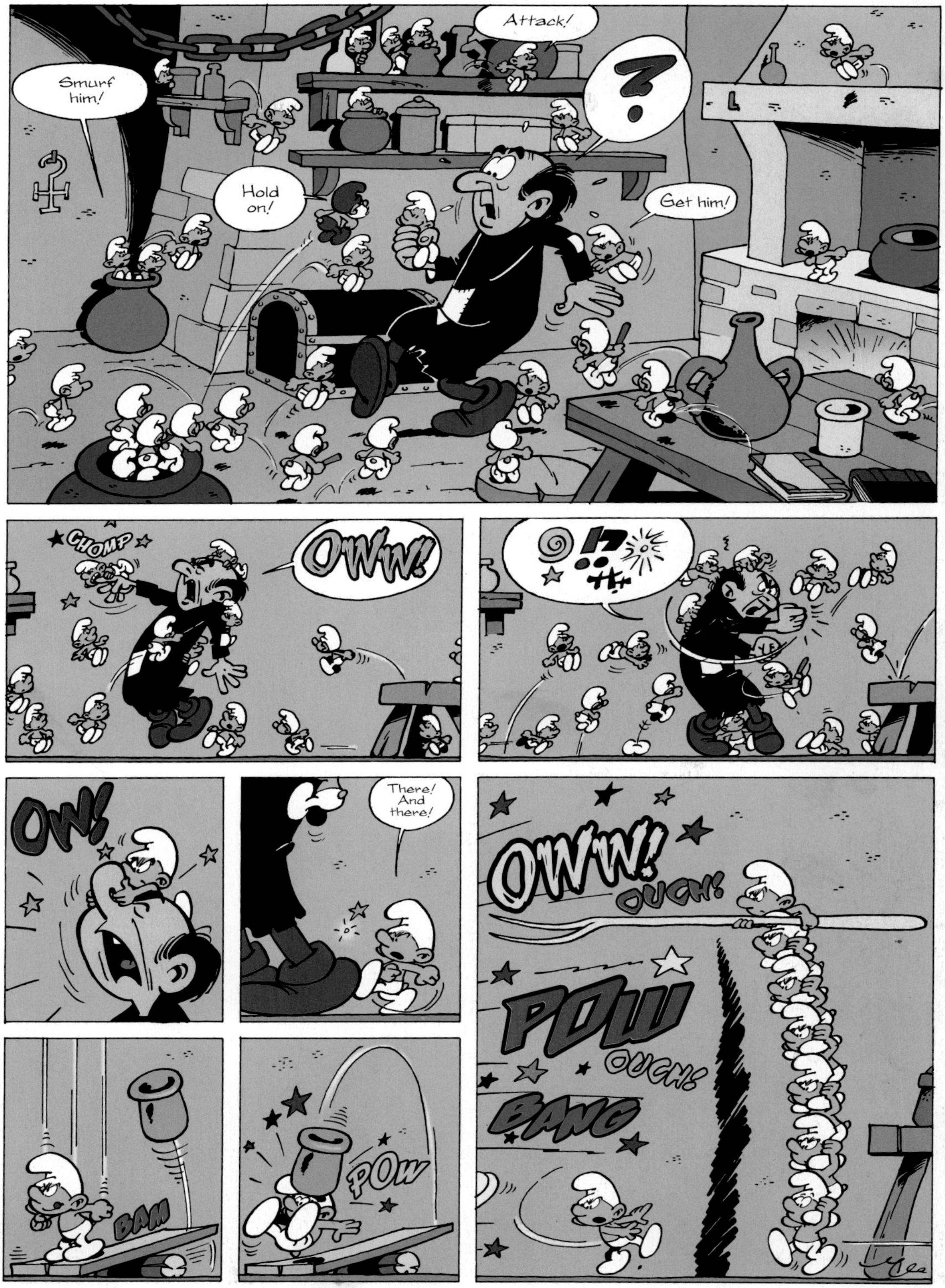

Smurf him!
Attack!
?
Hold on!
Get him!
CHOMP
OWW!
OW!
There! And there!
OWW!
OUCH!
POW
OUCH!
BANG
BAM
POW

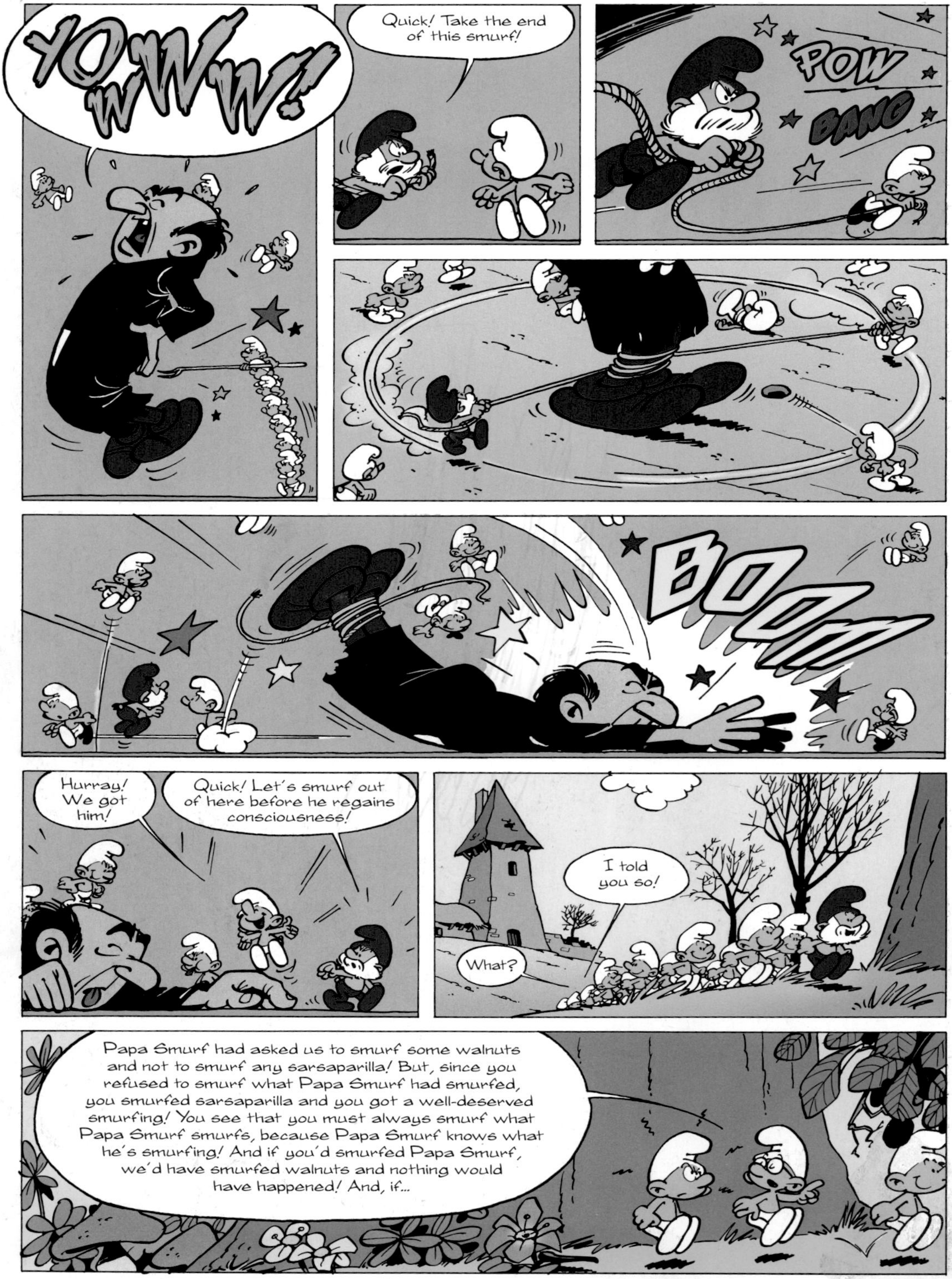
YOWWWW!
Quick! Take the end of this smurf!
POW
BANG
BOOM
Hurray! We got him!
Quick! Let's smurf out of here before he regains consciousness!
I told you so!
What?
Papa Smurf had asked us to smurf some walnuts and not to smurf any sarsaparilla! But, since you refused to smurf what Papa Smurf had smurfed, you smurfed sarsaparilla and you got a well-deserved smurfing! You see that you must always smurf what Papa Smurf smurfs, because Papa Smurf knows what he's smurfing! And if you'd smurfed Papa Smurf, we'd have smurfed walnuts and nothing would have happened! And, if...

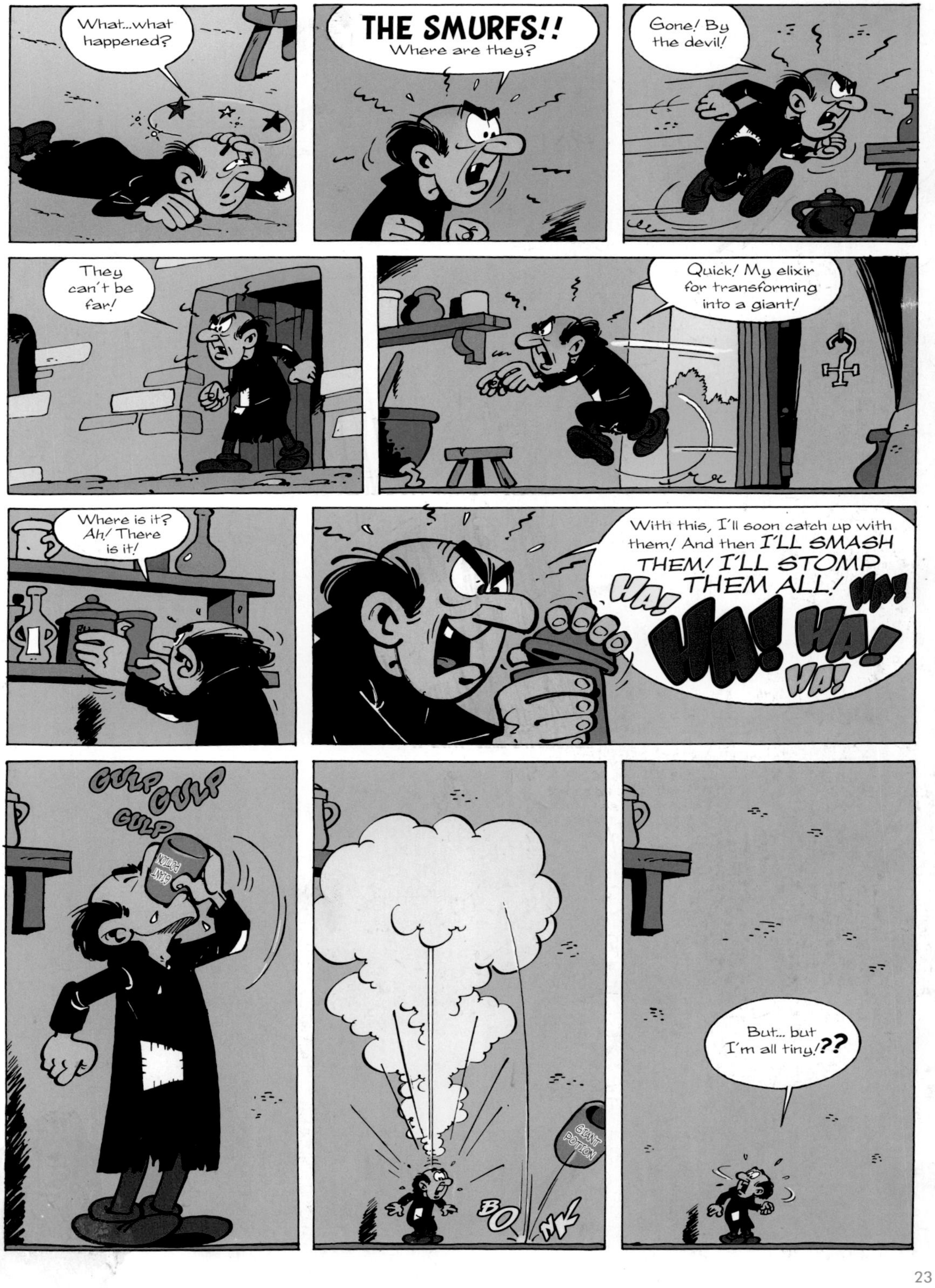

What...what happened?
THE SMURFS!! Where are they?
Gone! By the devil!
They can't be far!
Quick! My elixir for transforming into a giant!
Where is it? Ah! There is it!
With this, I'll soon catch up with them! And then I'LL SMASH THEM! I'LL STOMP THEM ALL!
HA! HA! HA! HA! HA!
GULP GULP GULP
GIANT POTION
GIANT POTION
BONK
But... but I'm all tiny!??

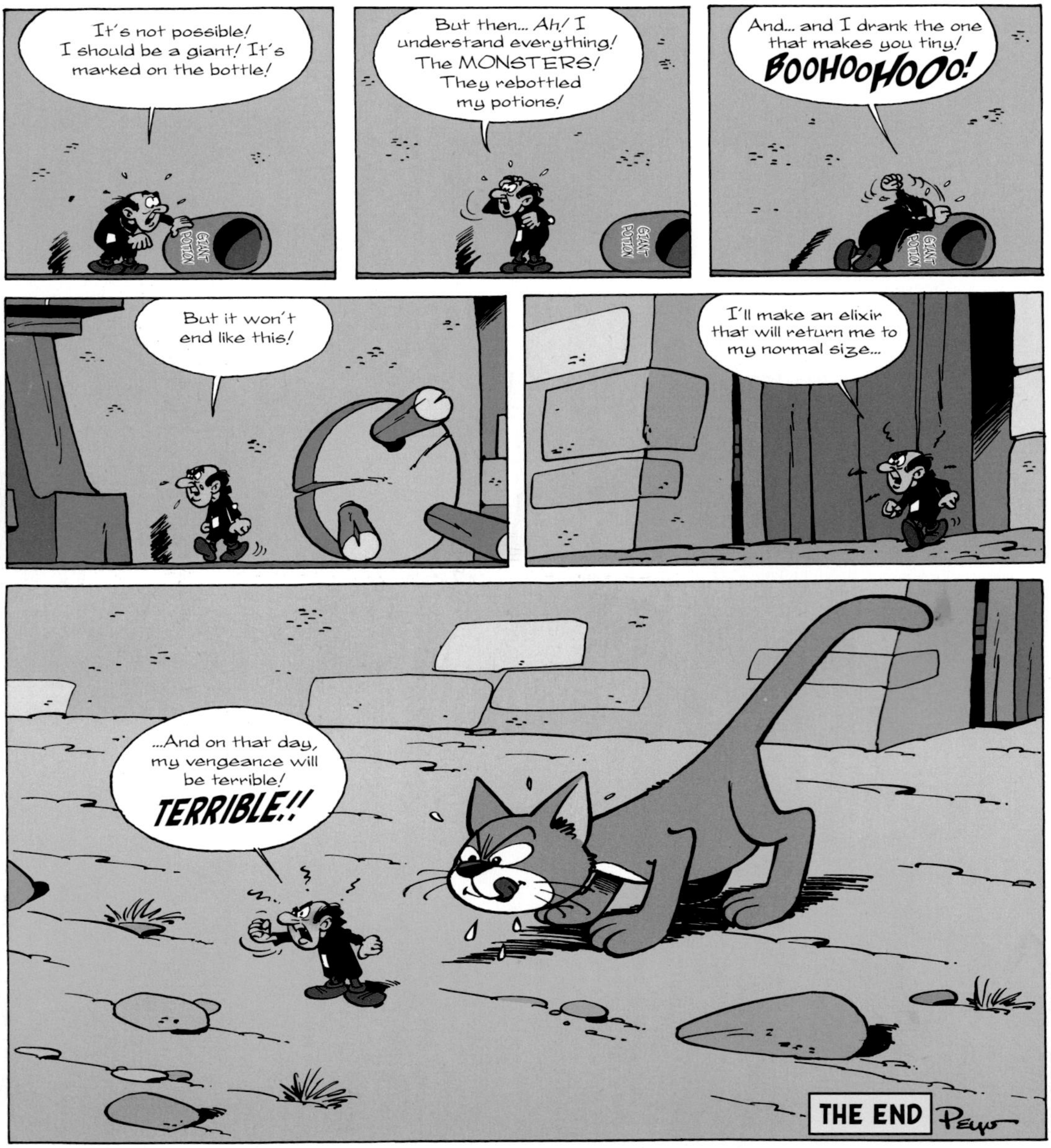
It's not possible! I should be a giant! It's marked on the bottle!
GIANT POTION
But then... Ah! I understand everything! The MONSTERS! They rebottled my potions!
GIANT POTION
And... and I drank the one that makes you tiny! BOOHOOHOOO!
GIANT POTION
But it won't end like this!
I'll make an elixir that will return me to my normal size...
...And on that day, my vengeance will be terrible! TERRIBLE!!
THE END
Peyo

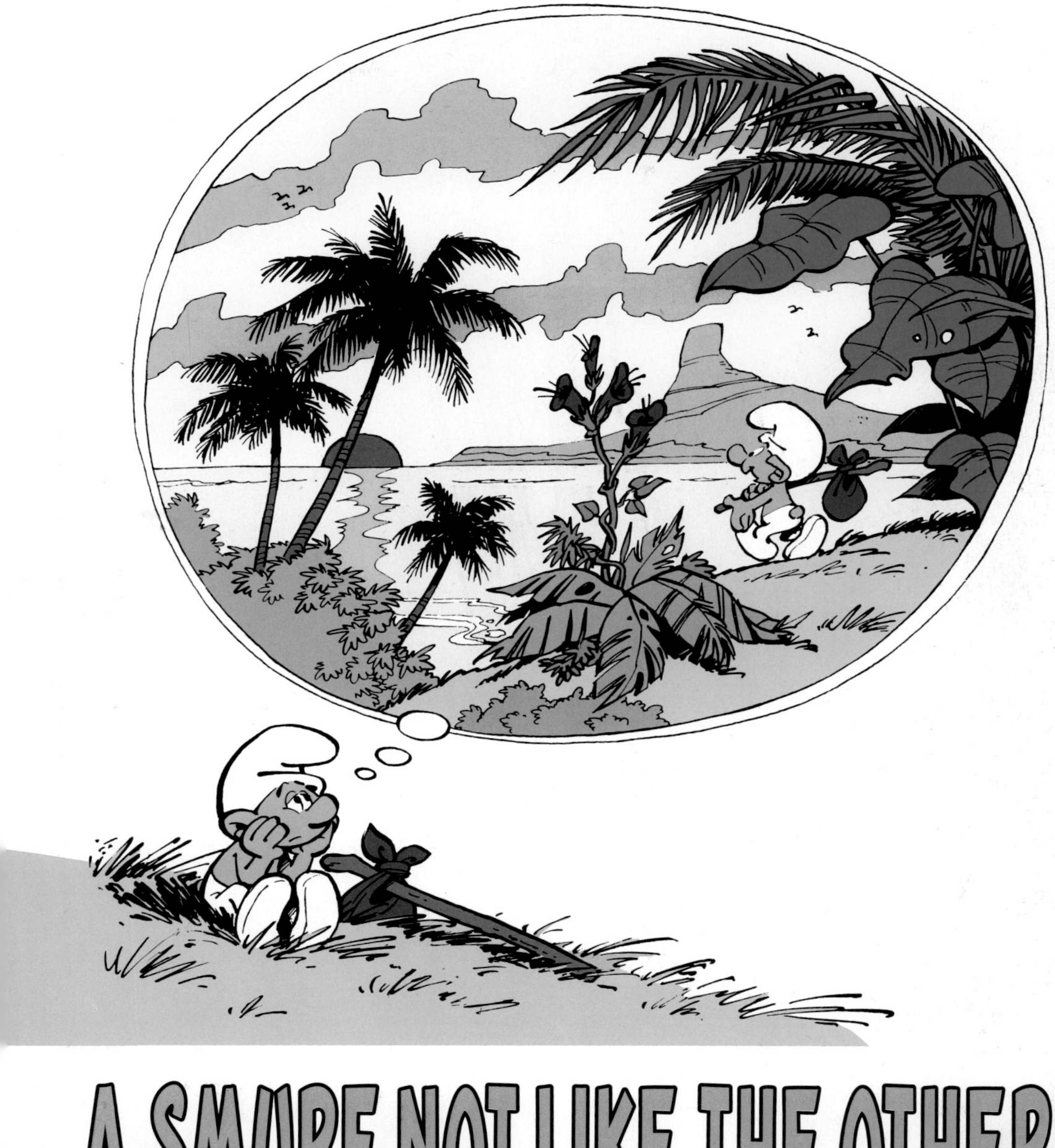

A SMURF NOT LIKE THE OTHERS

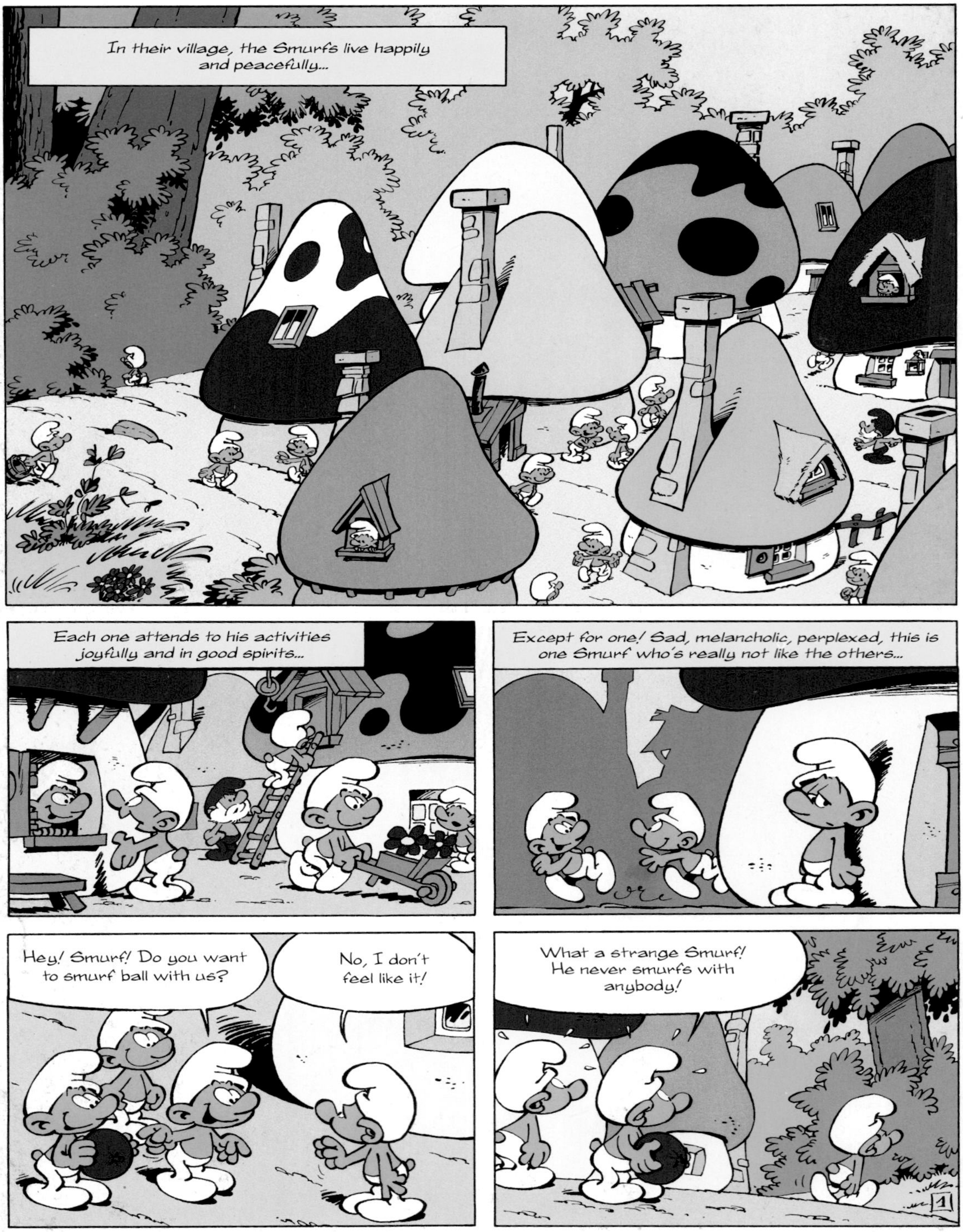
In their village, the Smurfs live happily and peacefully...
Each one attends to his activities joyfully and in good spirits...
Except for one! Sad, melancholic, perplexed, this is one Smurf who's really not like the others...
Hey! Smurf! Do you want to smurf ball with us?
No, I don't feel like it!
What a strange Smurf! He never smurfs with anybody!
1

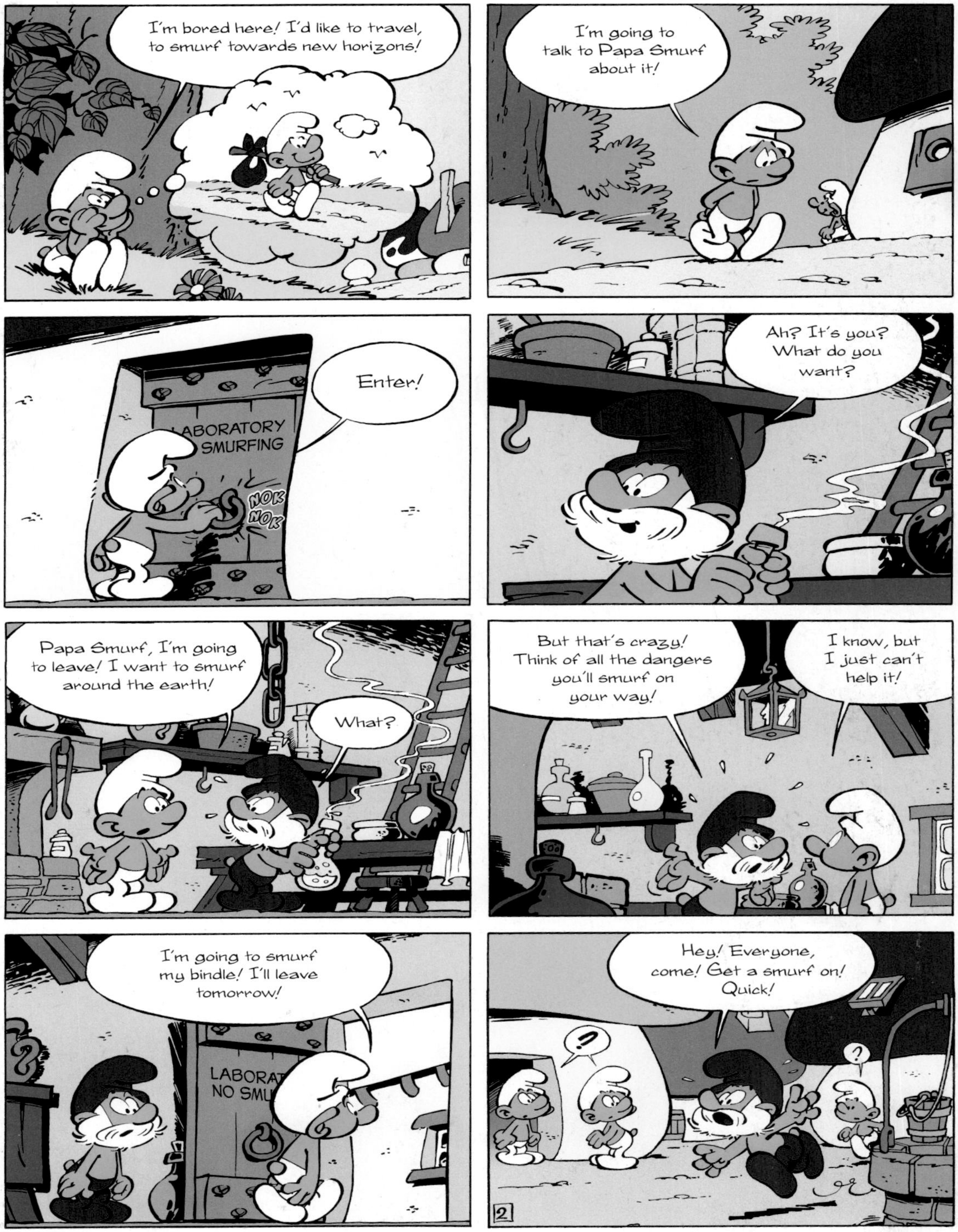
I'm bored here! I'd like to travel, to smurf towards new horizons!
I'm going to talk to Papa Smurf about it!
LABORATORY SMURFING
NOK NOK
Enter!
Ah? It's you? What do you want?
Papa Smurf, I'm going to leave! I want to smurf around the earth!
What?
But that's crazy! Think of all the dangers you'll smurf on your way!
I know, but I just can't help it!
I'm going to smurf my bindle! I'll leave tomorrow!
Hey! Everyone, come! Get a smurf on! Quick!
?!
?
2

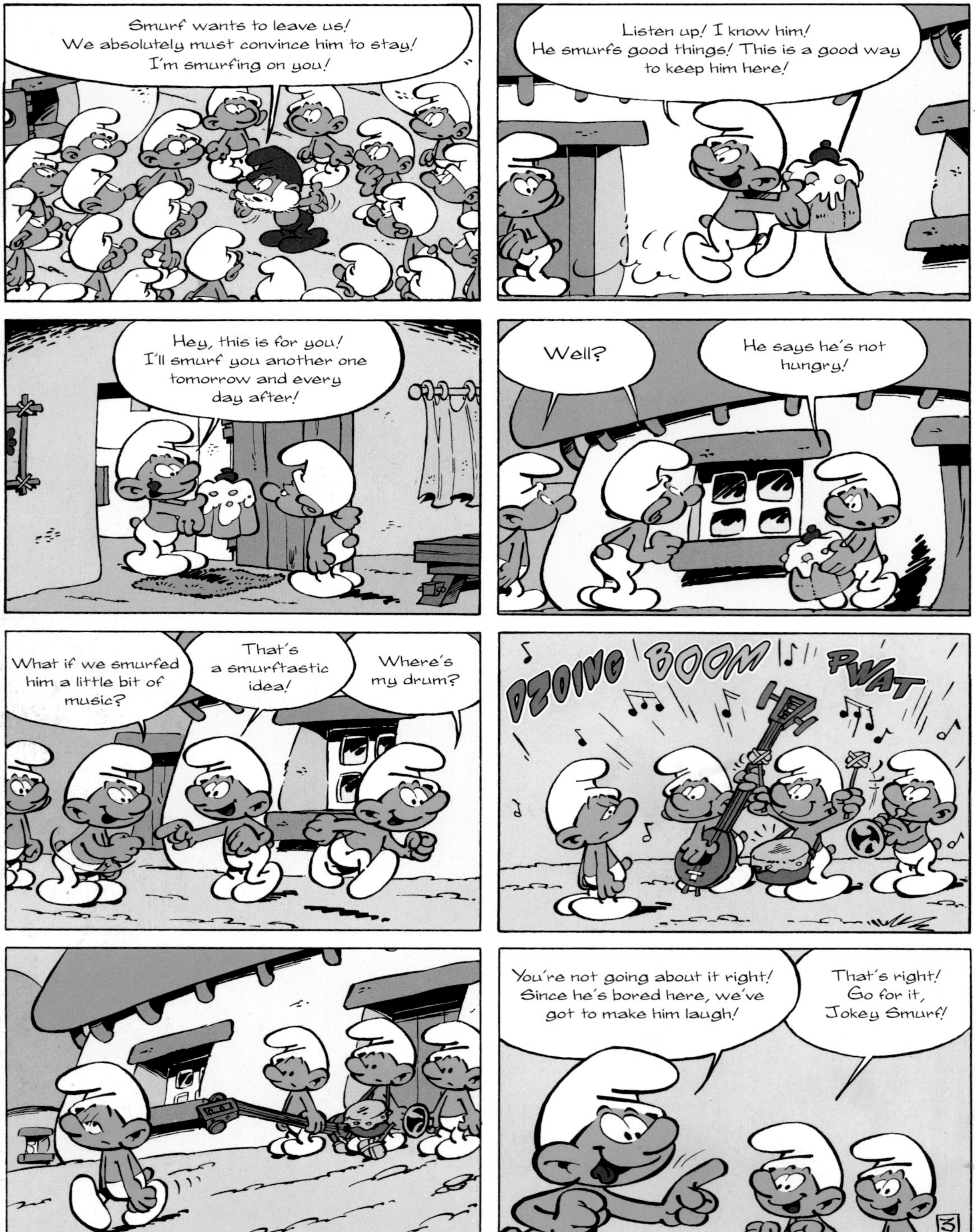
Smurf wants to leave us! We absolutely must convince him to stay! I'm smurfing on you!
Listen up! I know him! He smurfs good things! This is a good way to keep him here!
Hey, this is for you! I'll smurf you another one tomorrow and every day after!
Well?
He says he's not hungry!
What if we smurfed him a little bit of music?
That's a smurftastic idea!
Where's my drum?
DZOING
BOOM
PWAT
You're not going about it right! Since he's bored here, we've got to make him laugh!
That's right! Go for it, Jokey Smurf!

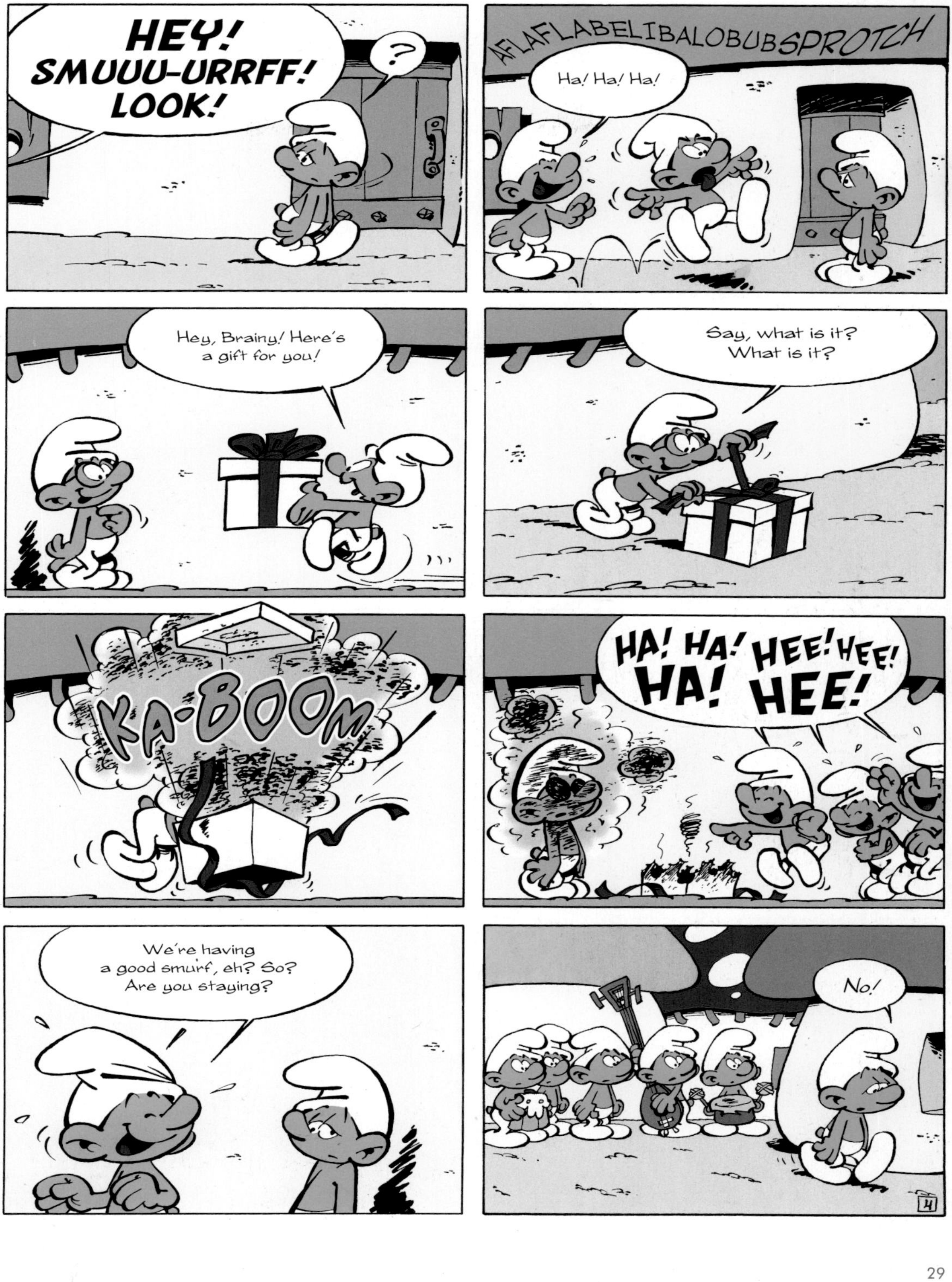

HEY! SMUUU-URRFF! LOOK!
?
AFLAFLABELIBALOBUBSPROTCH
Ha! Ha! Ha!
Hey, Brainy! Here's a gift for you!
Say, what is it? What is it?
KA-BOOM
HA! HA! HA! HEE! HEE! HEE!
We're having a good smurf, eh? So? Are you staying?
No!

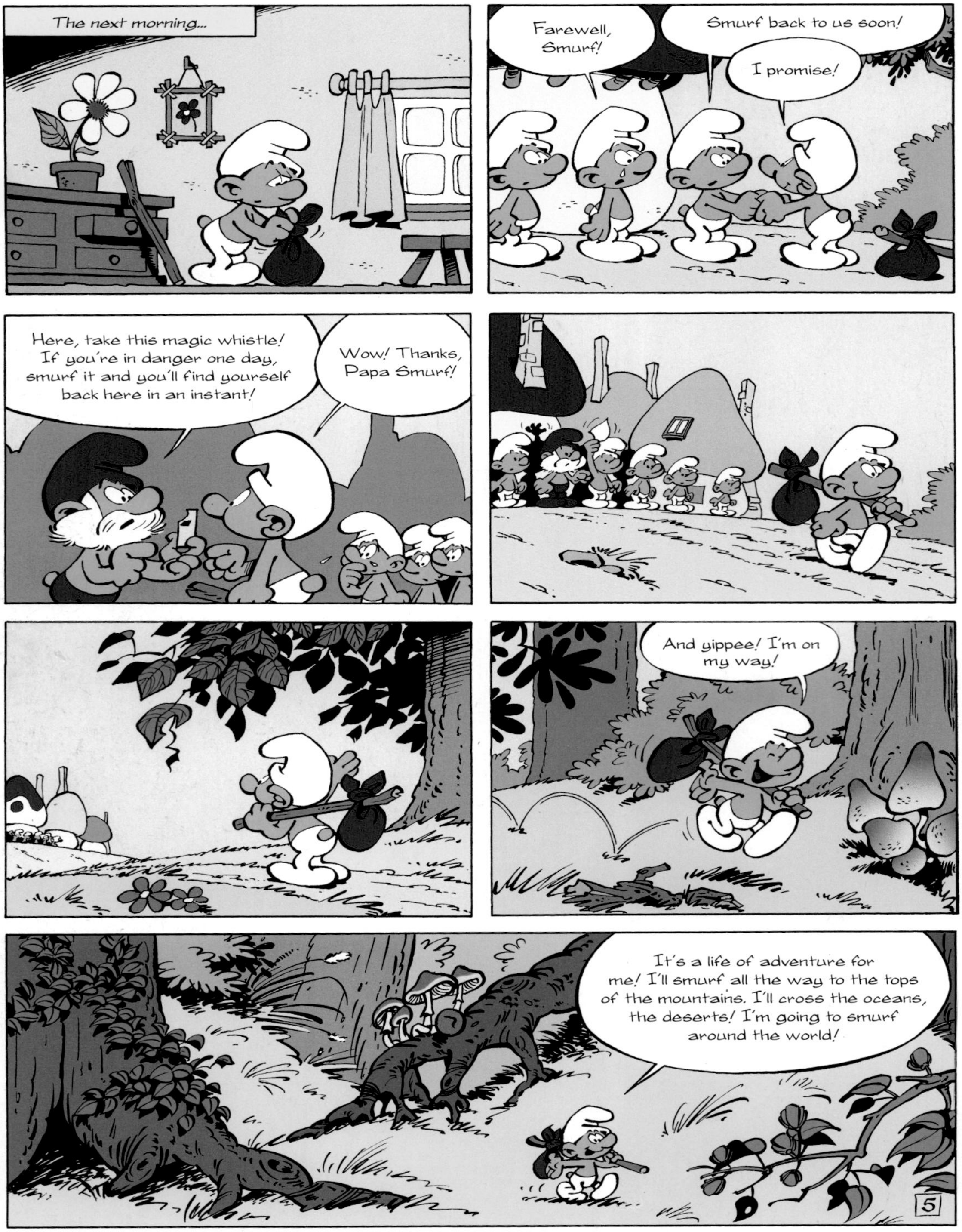
The next morning...
Farewell, Smurf!
Smurf back to us soon!
I promise!
Here, take this magic whistle! If you're in danger one day, smurf it and you'll find yourself back here in an instant!
Wow! Thanks, Papa Smurf!
And yippee! I'm on my way!
It's a life of adventure for me! I'll smurf all the way to the tops of the mountains. I'll cross the oceans, the deserts! I'm going to smurf around the world!
5

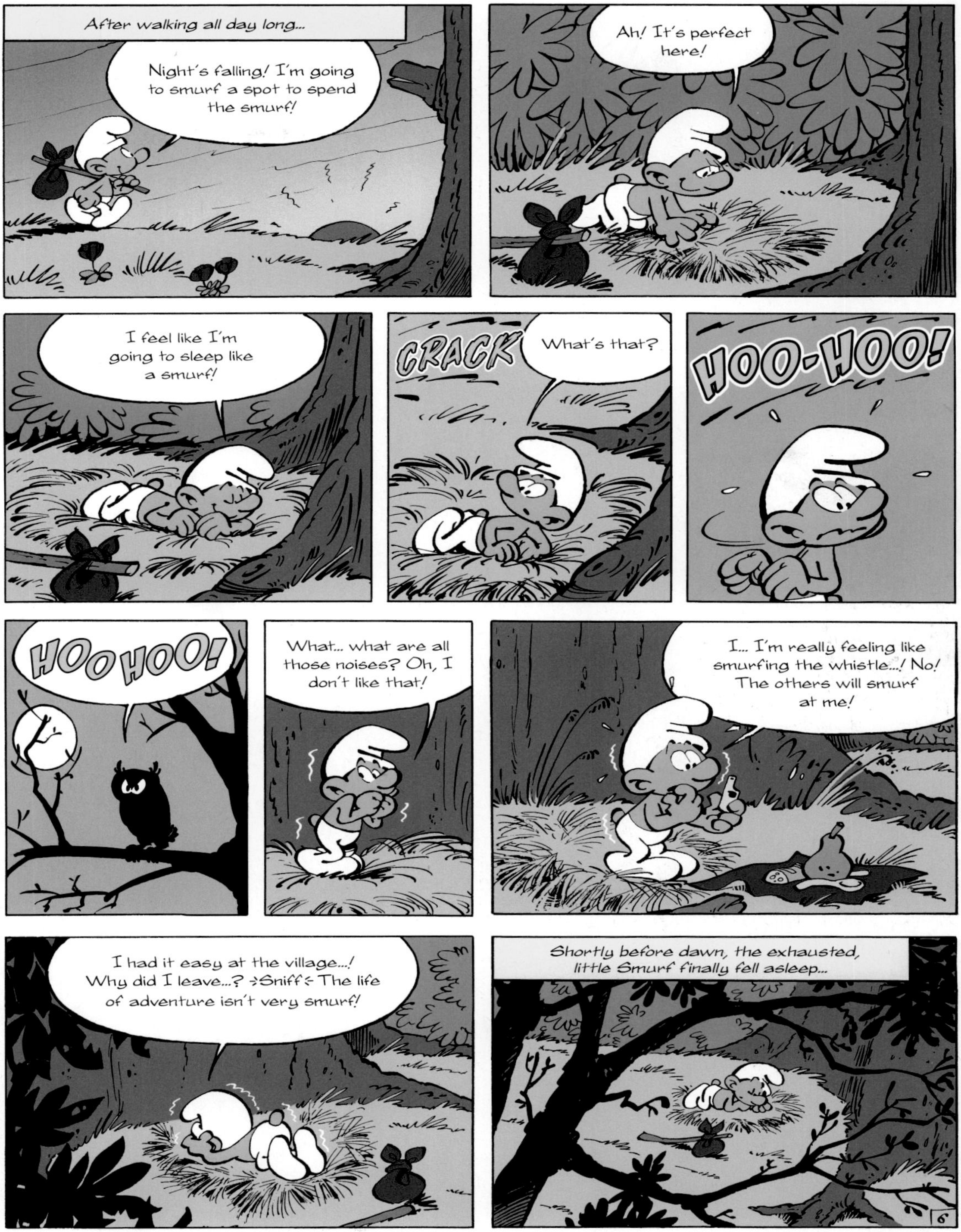
After walking all day long...
Night's falling! I'm going to smurf a spot to spend the smurf!
Ah! It's perfect here!
I feel like I'm going to sleep like a smurf!
CRACK
What's that?
HOO-HOO!
HOO HOO!
What... what are all those noises? Oh, I don't like that!
I... I'm really feeling like smurfing the whistle...! No! The others will smurf at me!
I had it easy at the village...! Why did I leave...? ⇥Sniff⇤ The life of adventure isn't very smurf!
Shortly before dawn, the exhausted, little Smurf finally fell asleep...
6

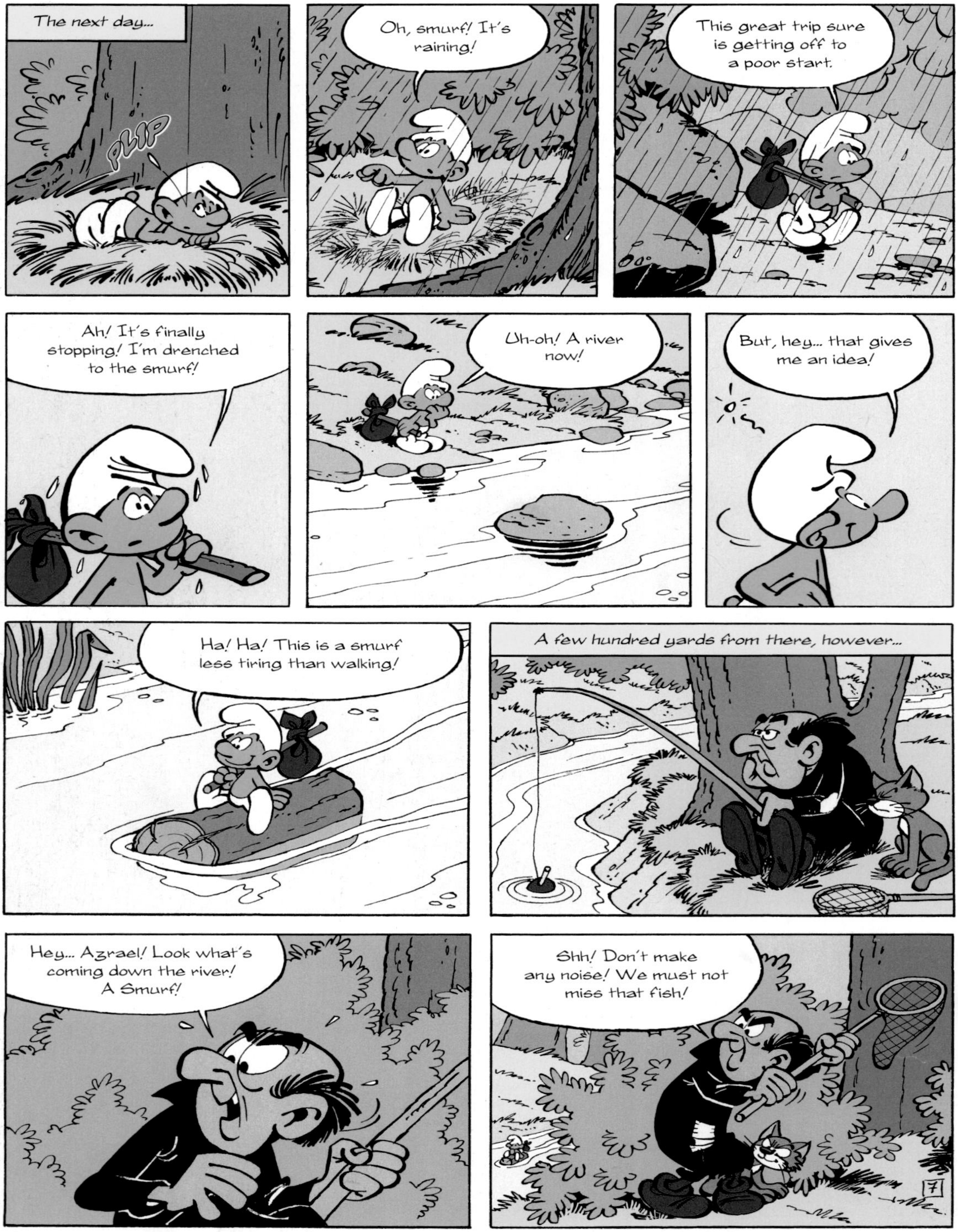
The next day...
PLIP
Oh, smurf! It's raining!
This great trip sure is getting off to a poor start.
Ah! It's finally stopping! I'm drenched to the smurf!
Uh-oh! A river now!
But, hey... that gives me an idea!
Ha! Ha! This is a smurf less tiring than walking!
A few hundred yards from there, however...
Hey... Azrael! Look what's coming down the river! A Smurf!
Shh! Don't make any noise! We must not miss that fish!
7

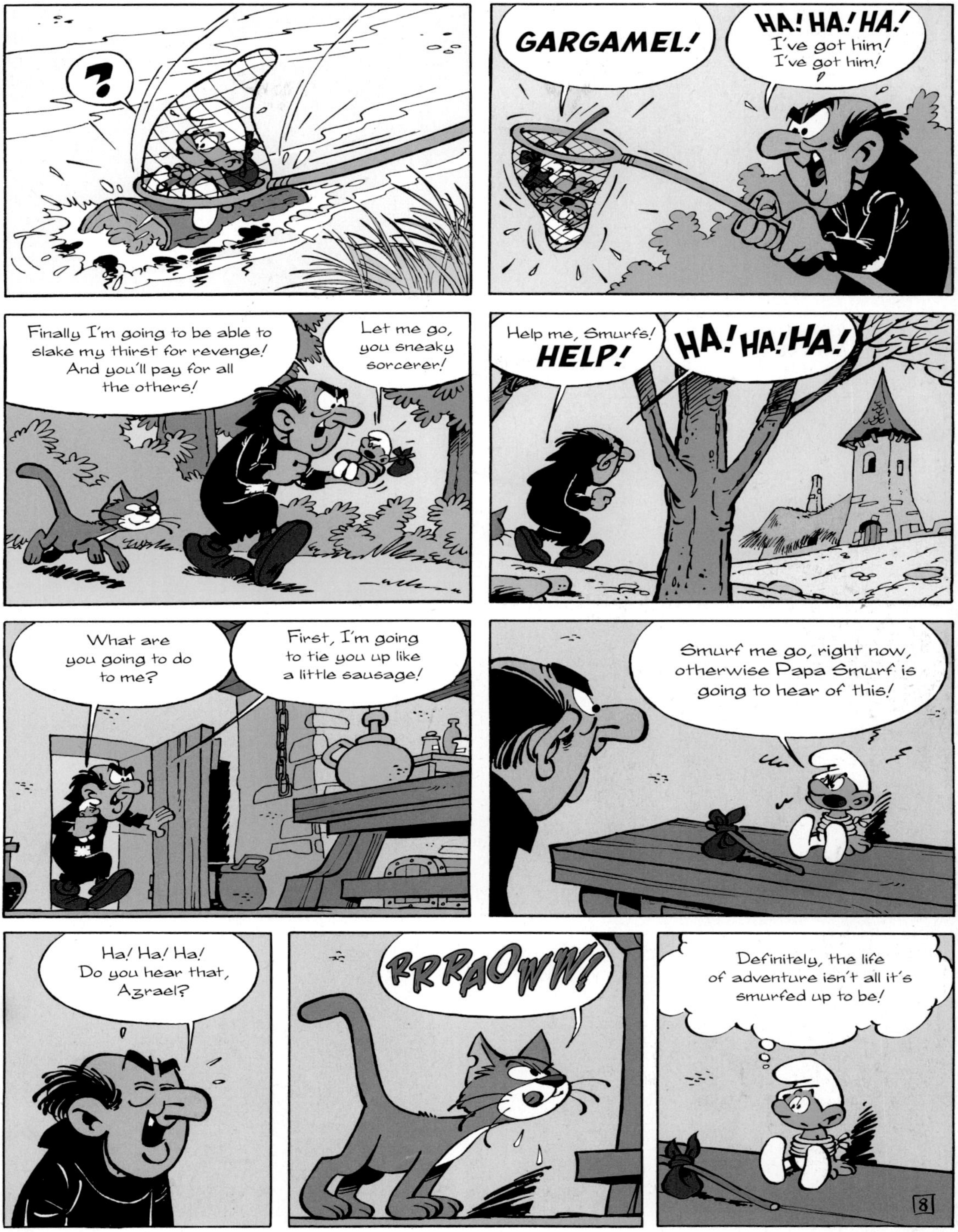
?
GARGAMEL!
HA! HA! HA! I've got him! I've got him!
Finally I'm going to be able to slake my thirst for revenge! And you'll pay for all the others!
Let me go, you sneaky sorcerer!
Help me, Smurfs! HELP!
HA! HA! HA!
What are you going to do to me?
First, I'm going to tie you up like a little sausage!
Smurf me go, right now, otherwise Papa Smurf is going to hear of this!
Ha! Ha! Ha! Do you hear that, Azrael?
RRRAOWW!
Definitely, the life of adventure isn't all it's smurfed up to be!
8

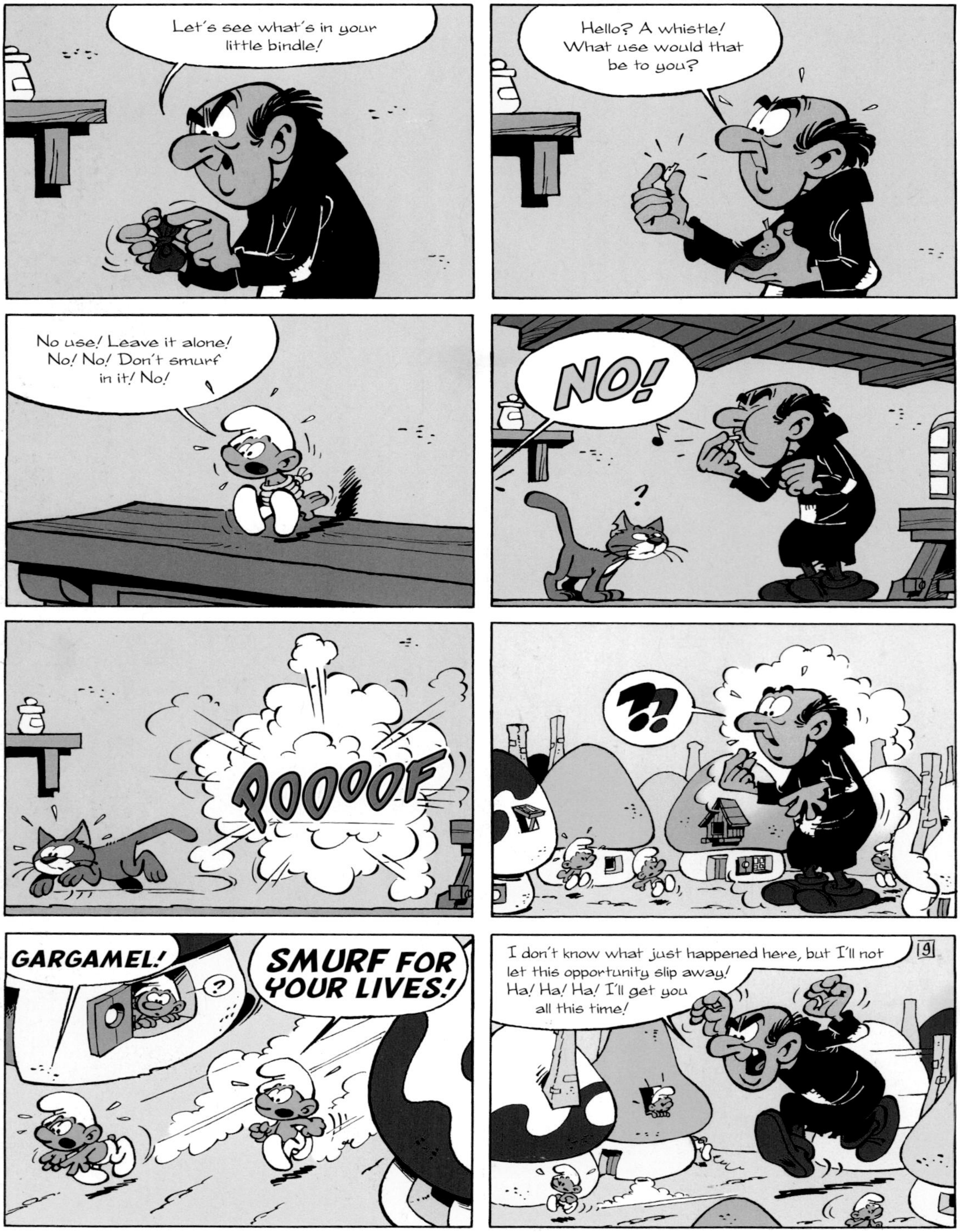
Let's see what's in your little bindle!
Hello? A whistle! What use would that be to you?
No use! Leave it alone! No! No! Don't smurf in it! No!
NO!
POOOOF
GARGAMEL!
?
SMURF FOR YOUR LIVES!
I don't know what just happened here, but I'll not let this opportunity slip away! Ha! Ha! Ha! I'll get you all this time!
19

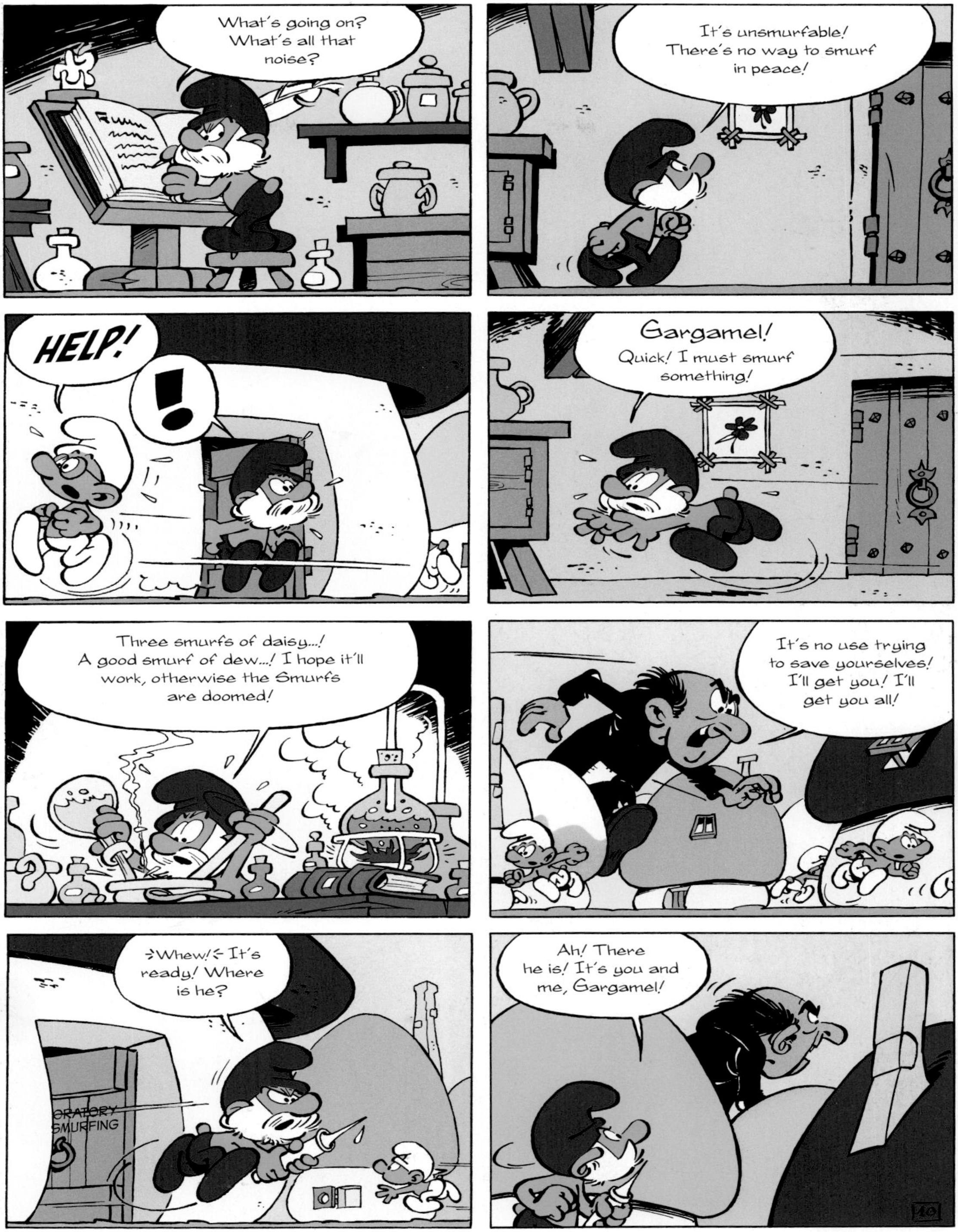
What's going on? What's all that noise?
It's unsmurfable! There's no way to smurf in peace!
HELP!
!
Gargamel! Quick! I must smurf something!
Three smurfs of daisy...! A good smurf of dew...! I hope it'll work, otherwise the Smurfs are doomed!
It's no use trying to save yourselves! I'll get you! I'll get you all!
Whew! It's ready! Where is he?
ORATORY
SMURFING
Ah! There he is! It's you and me, Gargamel!

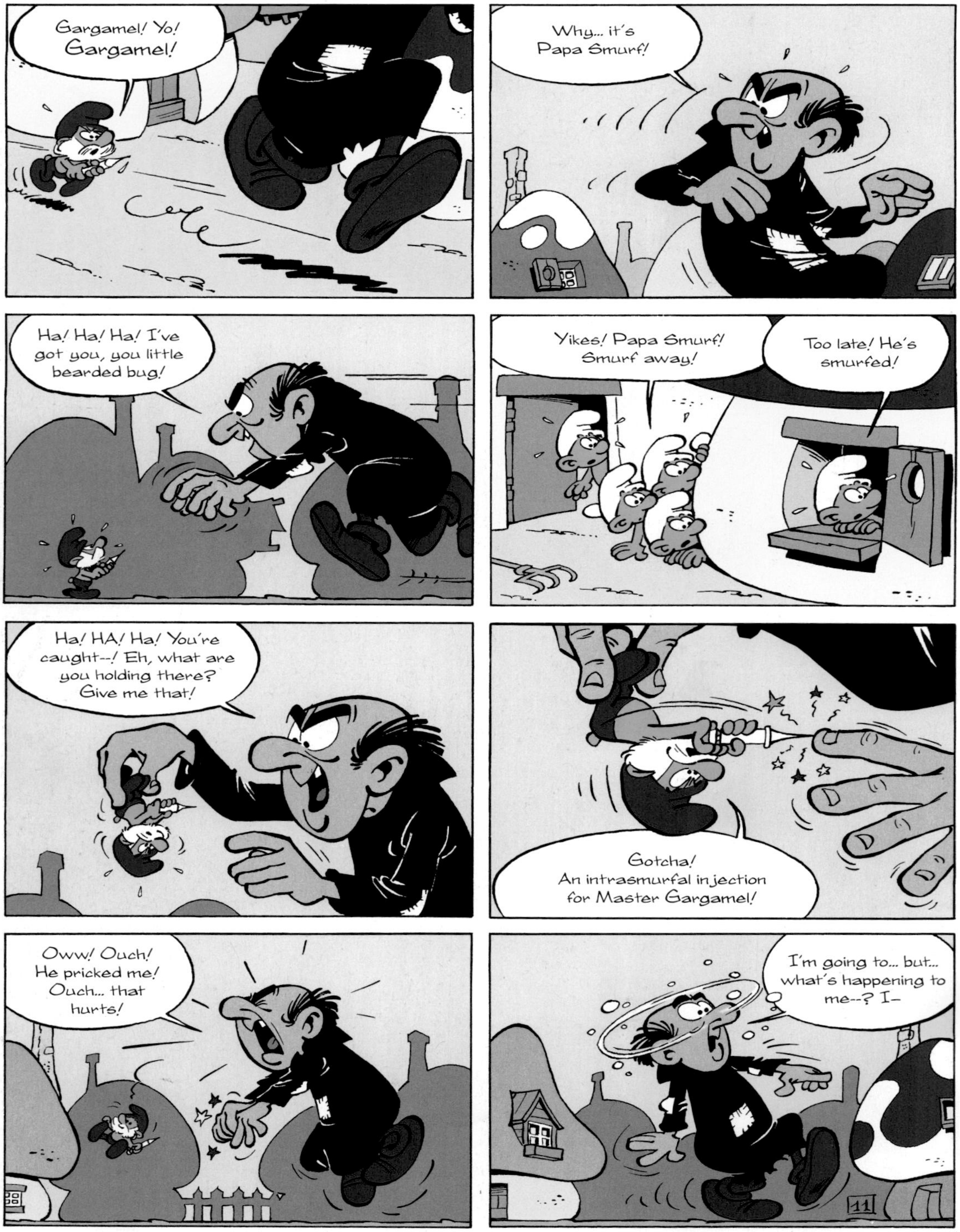
Gargamel! Yo! Gargamel!
Why... it's Papa Smurf!
Ha! Ha! Ha! I've got you, you little bearded bug!
Yikes! Papa Smurf! Smurf away!
Too late! He's smurfed!
Ha! HA! Ha! You're caught--! Eh, what are you holding there? Give me that!
Gotcha! An intrasmurfal injection for Master Gargamel!
Oww! Ouch! He pricked me! Ouch... that hurts!
I'm going to... but... what's happening to me--? I–
11

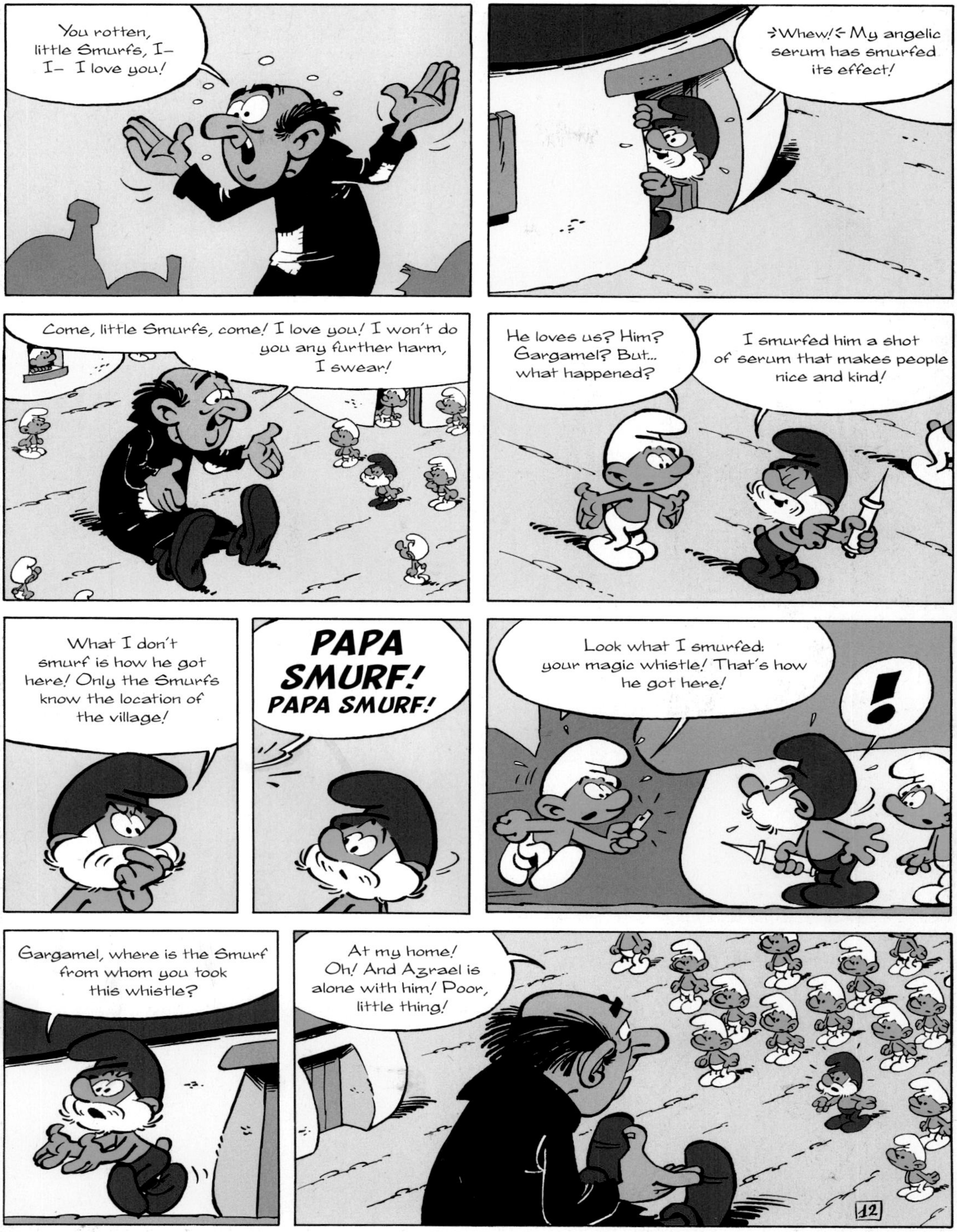
You rotten, little Smurfs, I– I– I love you!
→Whew!← My angelic serum has smurfed its effect!
Come, little Smurfs, come! I love you! I won't do you any further harm, I swear!
He loves us? Him? Gargamel? But... what happened?
I smurfed him a shot of serum that makes people nice and kind!
What I don't smurf is how he got here! Only the Smurfs know the location of the village!
PAPA SMURF! PAPA SMURF!
Look what I smurfed: your magic whistle! That's how he got here!
!
Gargamel, where is the Smurf from whom you took this whistle?
At my home! Oh! And Azrael is alone with him! Poor, little thing!
12

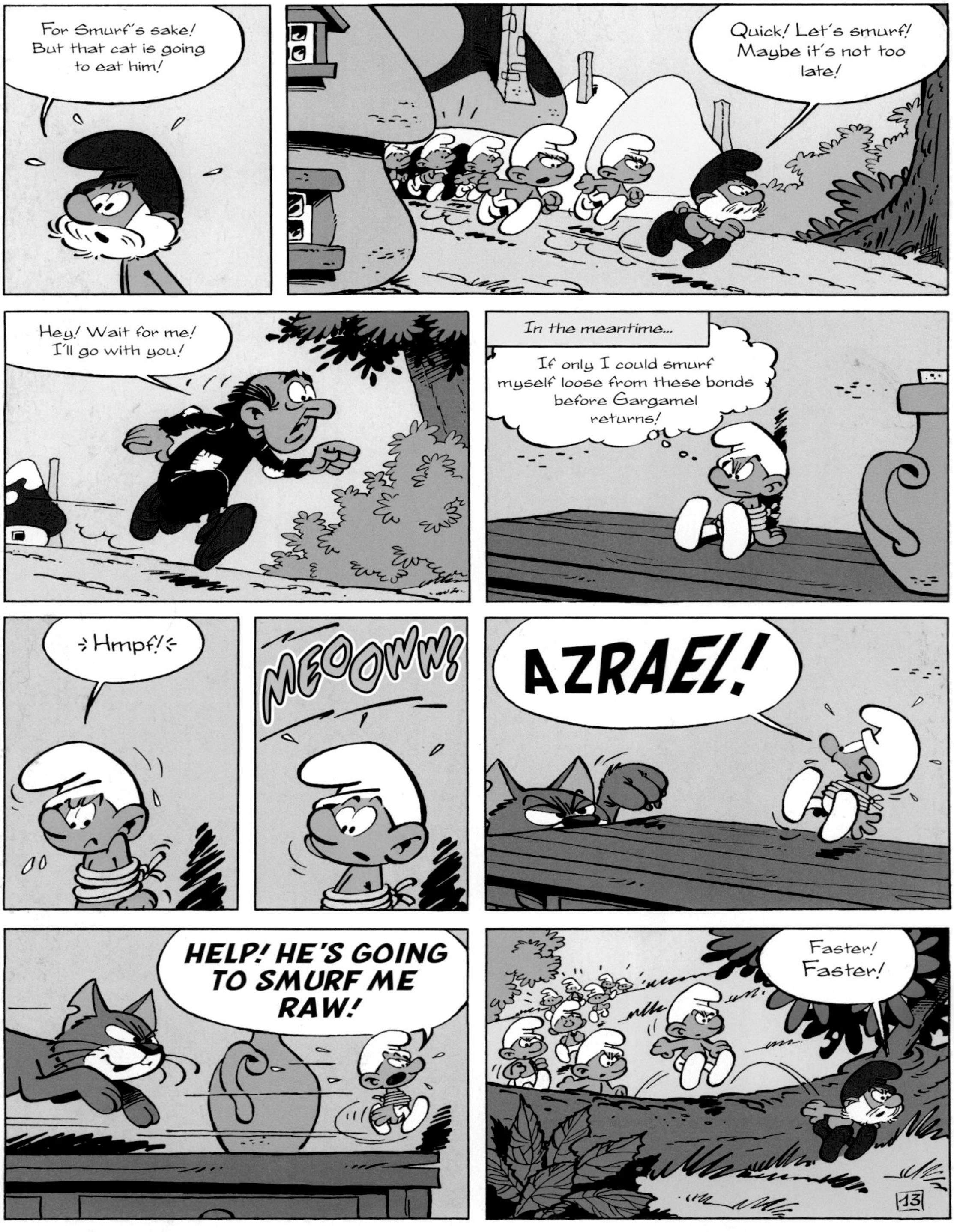
For Smurf's sake! But that cat is going to eat him!
Quick! Let's smurf! Maybe it's not too late!
Hey! Wait for me! I'll go with you!
In the meantime...
If only I could smurf myself loose from these bonds before Gargamel returns!
Hmpf!
MEOOWW!
AZRAEL!
HELP! HE'S GOING TO SMURF ME RAW!
Faster! Faster!
13

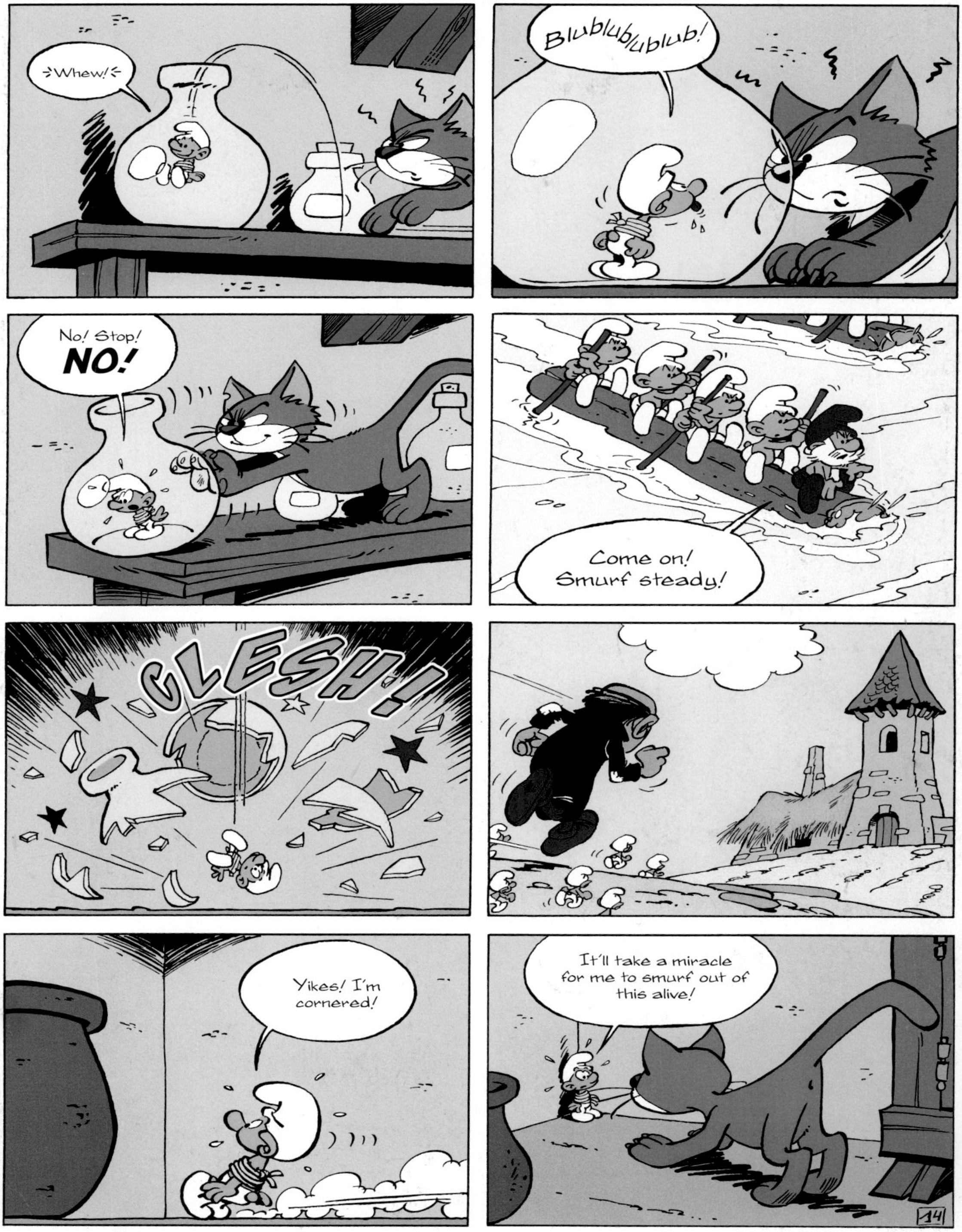
Whew!
Blublublublub!
No! Stop! NO!
Come on! Smurf steady!
CLESH!
Yikes! I'm cornered!
It'll take a miracle for me to smurf out of this alive!
14

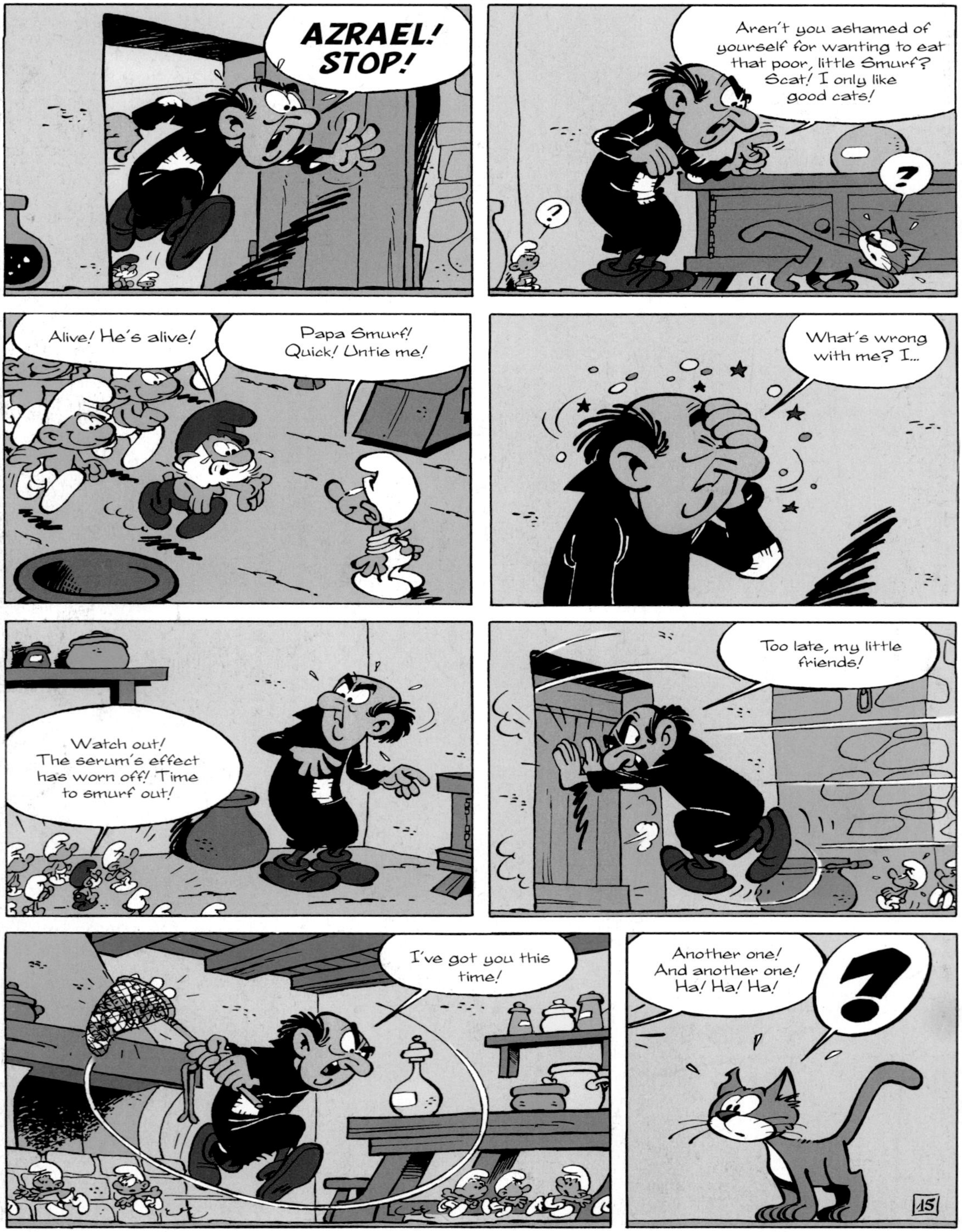
AZRAEL! STOP!
Aren't you ashamed of yourself for wanting to eat that poor, little Smurf? Scat! I only like good cats!
?
?
Alive! He's alive!
Papa Smurf! Quick! Untie me!
What's wrong with me? I...
Watch out! The serum's effect has worn off! Time to smurf out!
Too late, my little friends!
I've got you this time!
Another one! And another one! Ha! Ha! Ha!
?
15

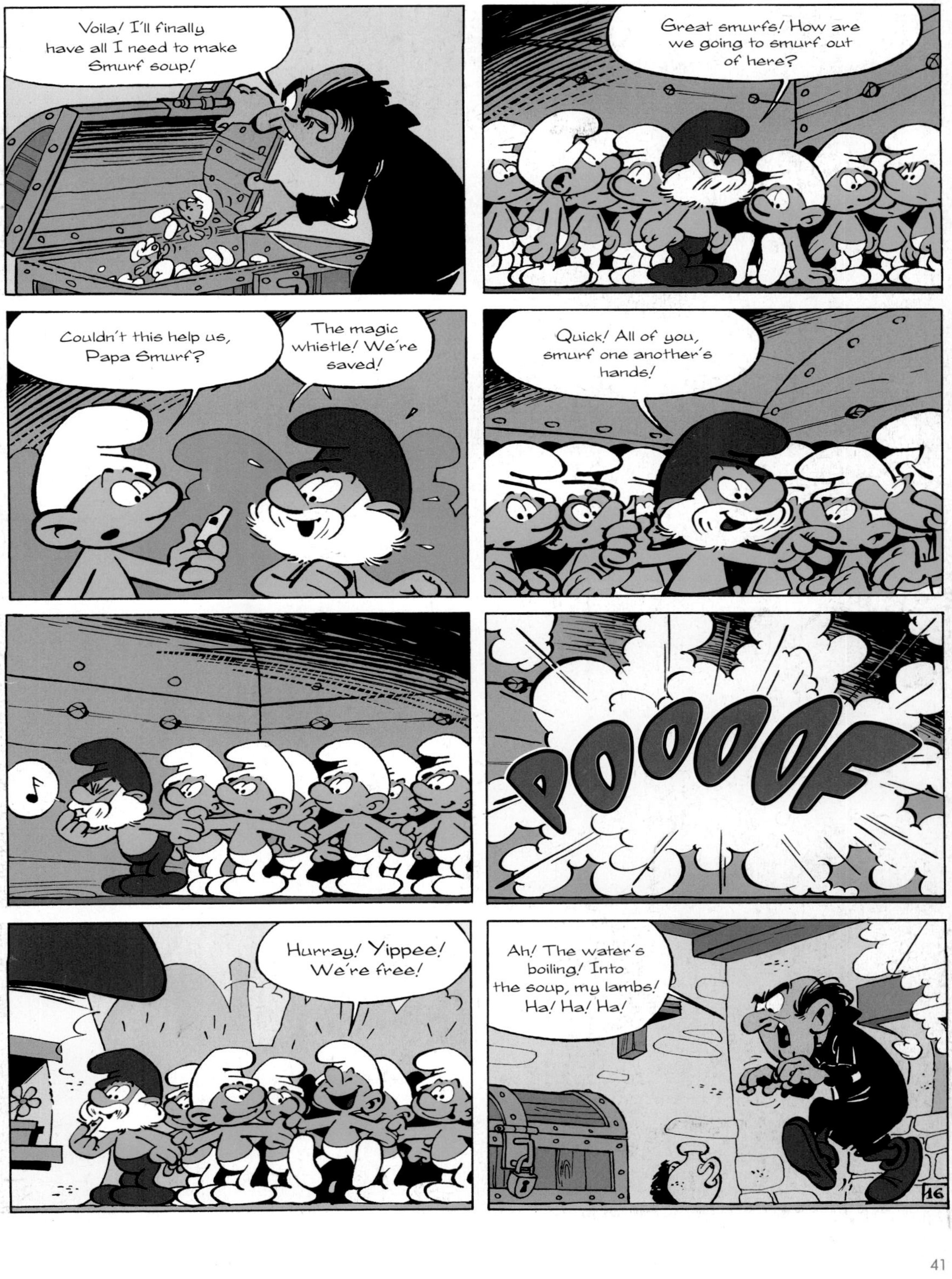
Voila! I'll finally have all I need to make Smurf soup!
Great smurfs! How are we going to smurf out of here?
Couldn't this help us, Papa Smurf?
The magic whistle! We're saved!
Quick! All of you, smurf one another's hands!
POOOOF
Hurray! Yippee! We're free!
Ah! The water's boiling! Into the soup, my lambs! Ha! Ha! Ha!
16

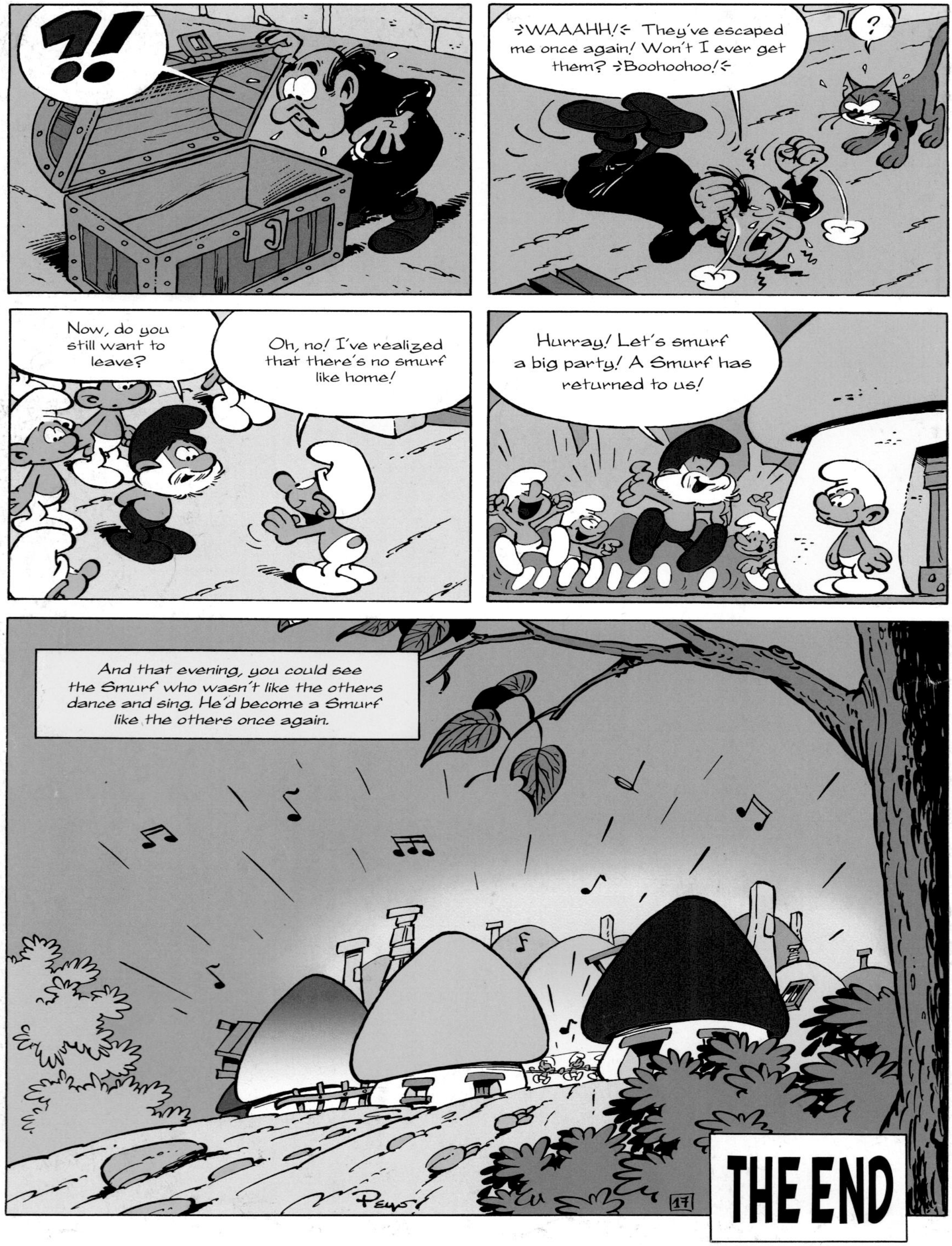
?!
>WAAAHH!< They've escaped me once again! Won't I ever get them? >Boohoohoo!<
?
Now, do you still want to leave?
Oh, no! I've realized that there's no smurf like home!
Hurray! Let's smurf a big party! A Smurf has returned to us!
And that evening, you could see the Smurf who wasn't like the others dance and sing. He'd become a Smurf like the others once again.
17
THE END

THE SMURFS AND THE LITTLE GHOST

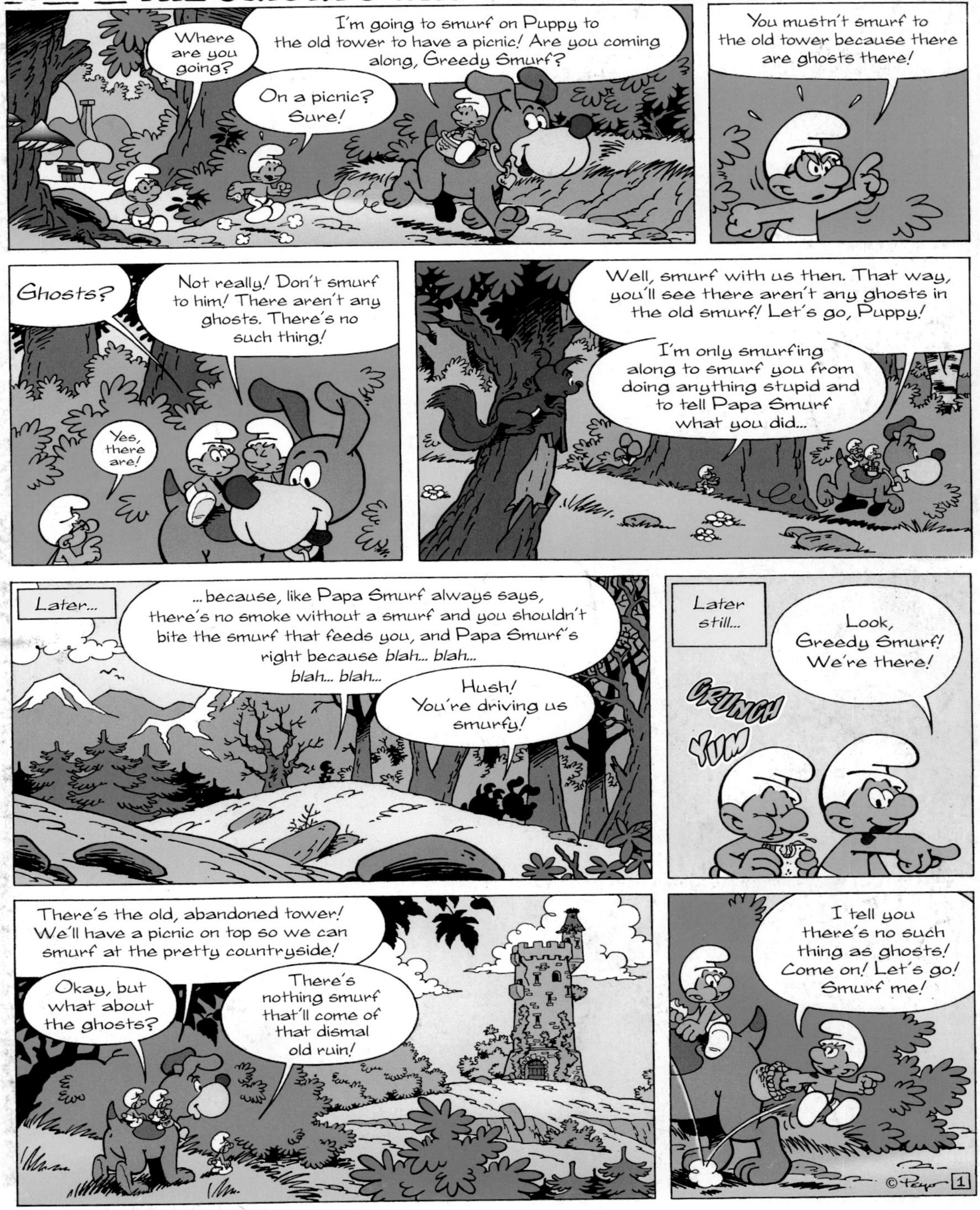

Where are you going?
I'm going to smurf on Puppy to the old tower to have a picnic! Are you coming along, Greedy Smurf?
On a picnic? Sure!
You mustn't smurf to the old tower because there are ghosts there!
Ghosts?
Not really! Don't smurf to him! There aren't any ghosts. There's no such thing!
Yes, there are!
Well, smurf with us then. That way, you'll see there aren't any ghosts in the old smurf! Let's go, Puppy!
I'm only smurfing along to smurf you from doing anything stupid and to tell Papa Smurf what you did...
Later...
...because, like Papa Smurf always says, there's no smoke without a smurf and you shouldn't bite the smurf that feeds you, and Papa Smurf's right because blah... blah... blah... blah...
Hush! You're driving us smurfy!
Later still...
Look, Greedy Smurf! We're there!
CRUNCH
YUM
There's the old, abandoned tower! We'll have a picnic on top so we can smurf at the pretty countryside!
Okay, but what about the ghosts?
There's nothing smurf that'll come of that dismal old ruin!
I tell you there's no such thing as ghosts! Come on! Let's go! Smurf me!
© Peyo
1

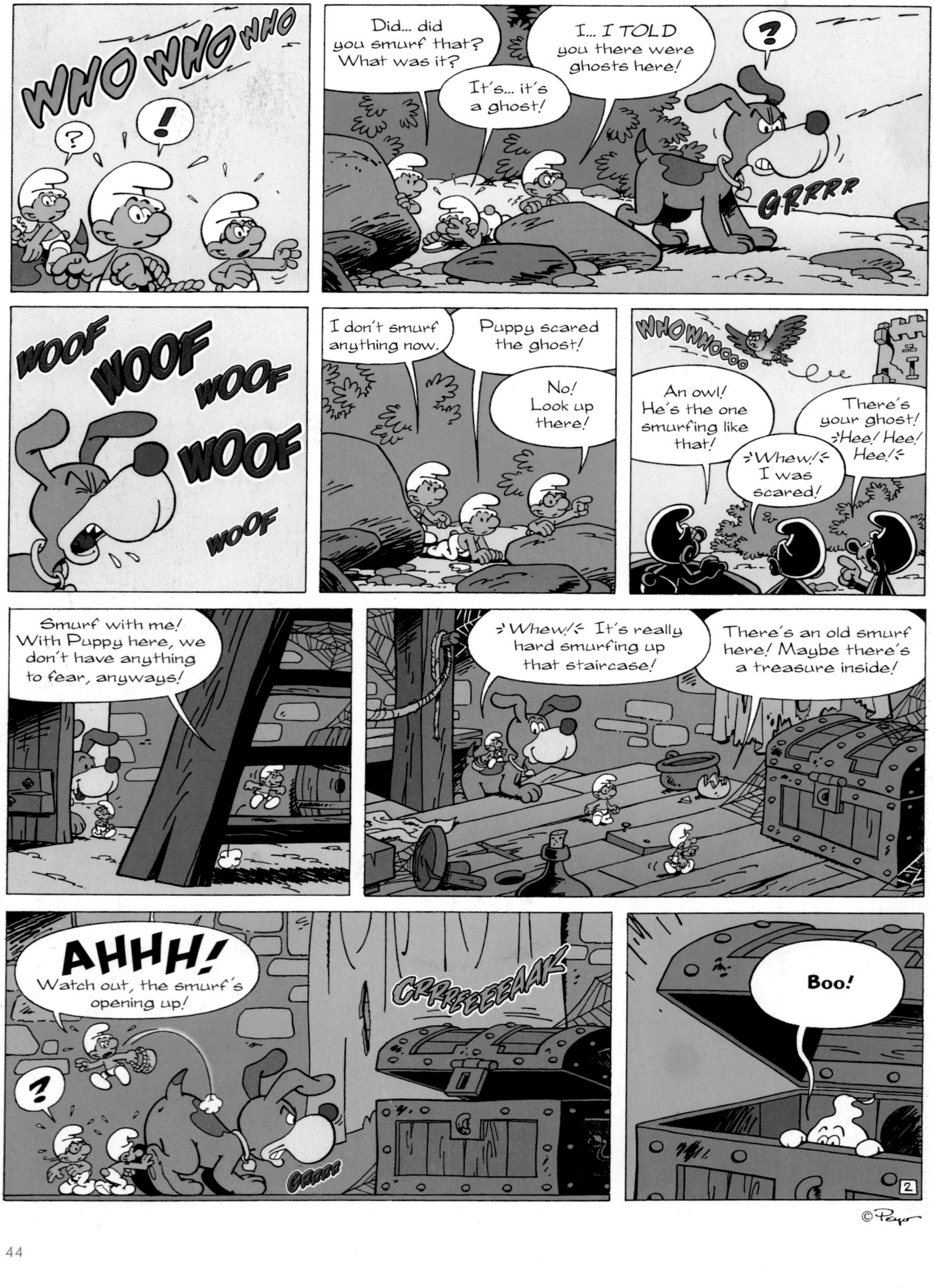
WHO WHO WHO
?
!
Did... did you smurf that? What was it?
It's... it's a ghost!
I... I TOLD you there were ghosts here!
?
GRRRR
WOOF WOOF WOOF WOOF WOOF
I don't smurf anything now.
Puppy scared the ghost!
No! Look up there!
WHO WHOOOO
An owl! He's the one smurfing like that!
Whew! I was scared!
There's your ghost! Hee! Hee! Hee!
Smurf with me! With Puppy here, we don't have anything to fear, anyways!
Whew! It's really hard smurfing up that staircase!
There's an old smurf here! Maybe there's a treasure inside!
AHHH! Watch out, the smurf's opening up!
CRRREEEEEAAK
?
GRRR
Boo!
2
© Peyo

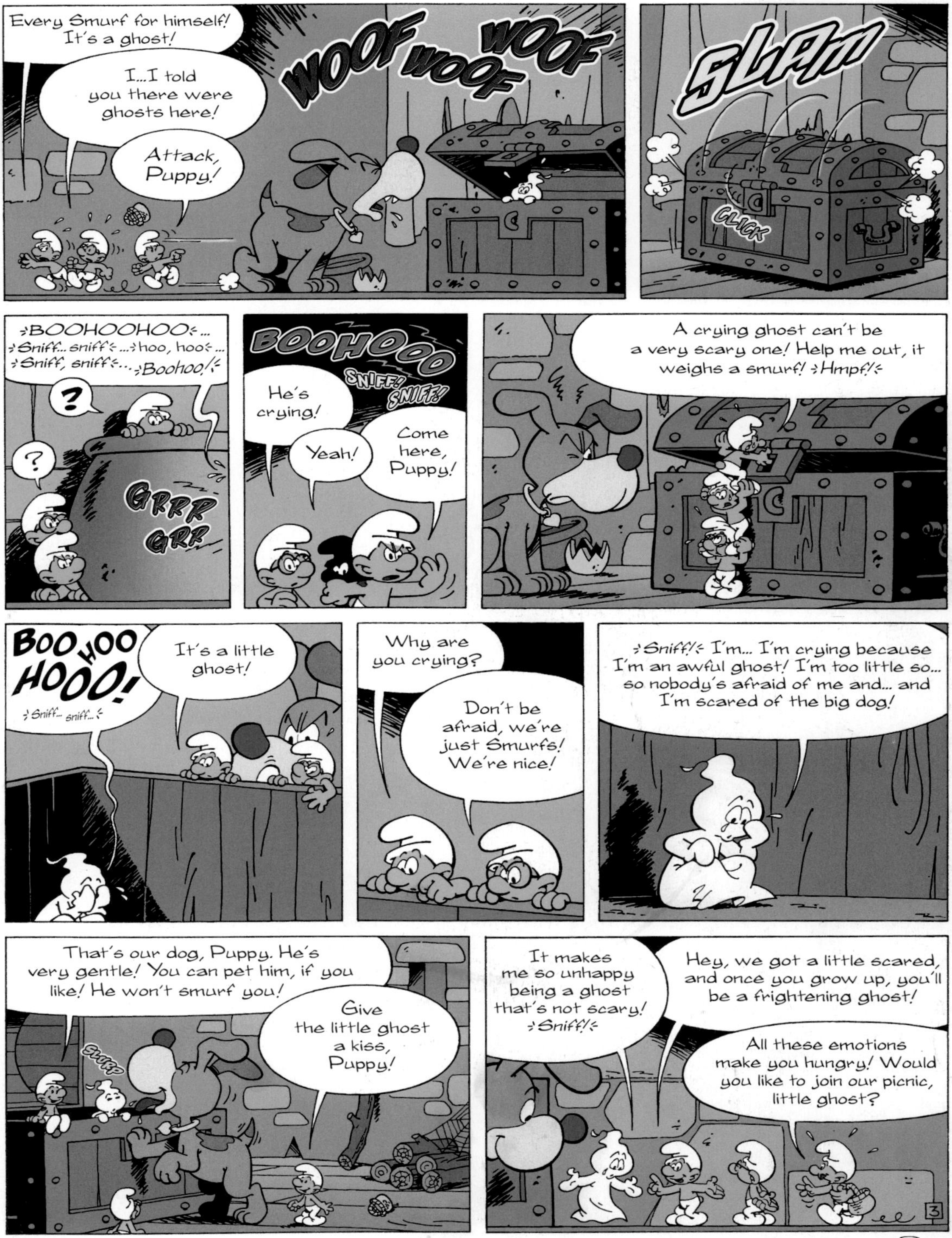

Every Smurf for himself! It's a ghost!
I...I told you there were ghosts here!
Attack, Puppy!
WOOF WOOF WOOF
SLAM
CLICK
BOOHOOHOO... Sniff... sniff... hoo, hoo... Sniff, sniff... Boohoo!
?
?
GRRR GRR
BOOHOOO
SNIFF! SNIFF!
He's crying!
Yeah!
Come here, Puppy!
A crying ghost can't be a very scary one! Help me out, it weighs a smurf! Hmpf!
BOO HOO HOOO!
Sniff... sniff...
It's a little ghost!
Why are you crying?
Don't be afraid, we're just Smurfs! We're nice!
Sniff! I'm... I'm crying because I'm an awful ghost! I'm too little so... so nobody's afraid of me and... and I'm scared of the big dog!
That's our dog, Puppy. He's very gentle! You can pet him, if you like! He won't smurf you!
SLURP
Give the little ghost a kiss, Puppy!
It makes me so unhappy being a ghost that's not scary! Sniff!
Hey, we got a little scared, and once you grow up, you'll be a frightening ghost!
All these emotions make you hungry! Would you like to join our picnic, little ghost?
3

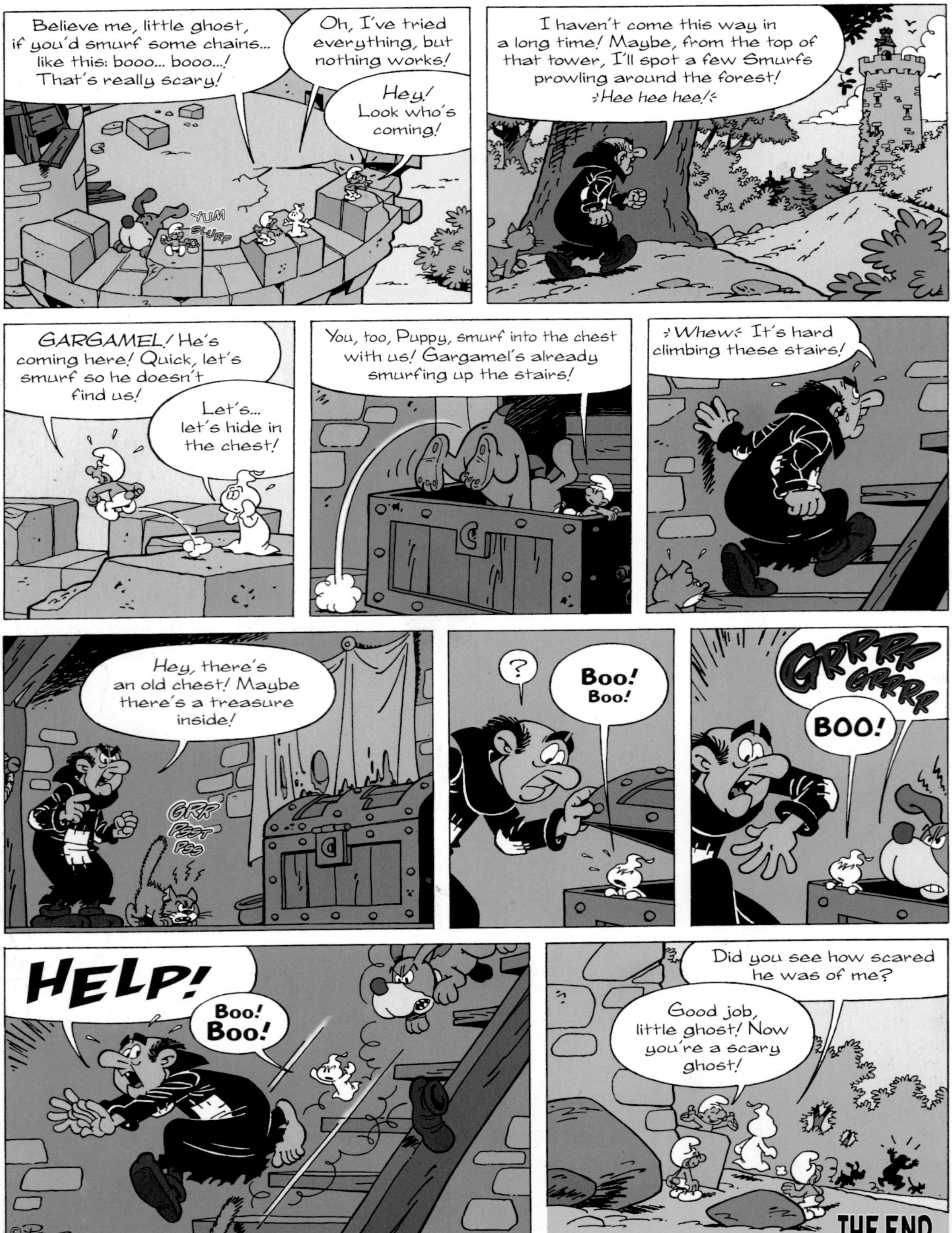
Believe me, little ghost, if you'd smurf some chains... like this: booo... booo...! That's really scary!
Oh, I've tried everything, but nothing works!
Hey! Look who's coming!
YUM
SLURP
I haven't come this way in a long time! Maybe, from the top of that tower, I'll spot a few Smurfs prowling around the forest! Hee hee hee!
GARGAMEL! He's coming here! Quick, let's smurf so he doesn't find us!
Let's... let's hide in the chest!
You, too, Puppy, smurf into the chest with us! Gargamel's already smurfing up the stairs!
Whew! It's hard climbing these stairs!
Hey, there's an old chest! Maybe there's a treasure inside!
GRR
PSST
PSS
?
Boo! Boo!
GRRRR GRRRR
BOO!
HELP!
Boo! Boo!
© Peyo
Did you see how scared he was of me?
Good job, little ghost! Now you're a scary ghost!
THE END

SAGRATAMABARB

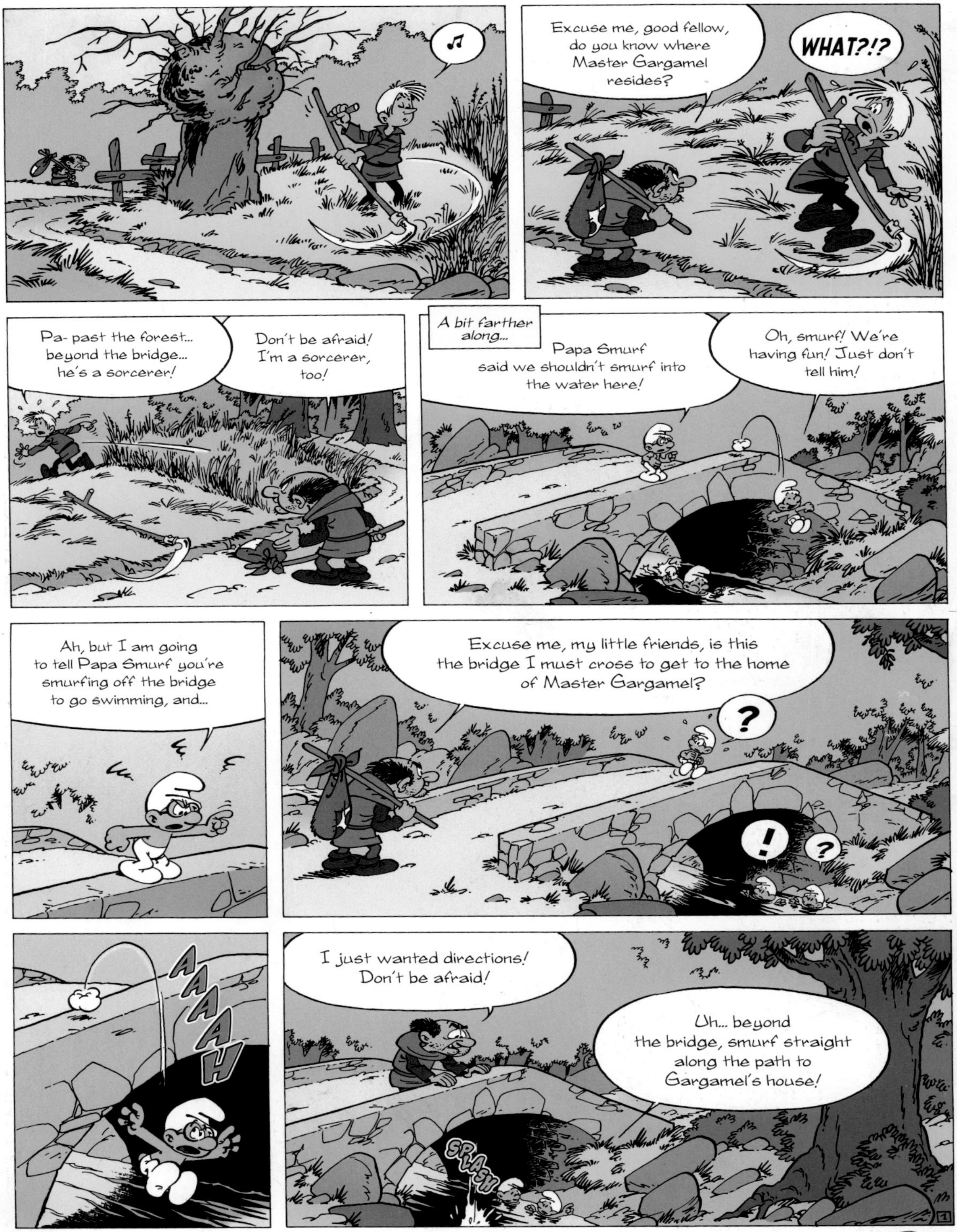
♪
Excuse me, good fellow, do you know where Master Gargamel resides?
WHAT?!?
Pa- past the forest... beyond the bridge... he's a sorcerer!
Don't be afraid! I'm a sorcerer, too!
A bit farther along...
Papa Smurf said we shouldn't smurf into the water here!
Oh, smurf! We're having fun! Just don't tell him!
Ah, but I am going to tell Papa Smurf you're smurfing off the bridge to go swimming, and...
Excuse me, my little friends, is this the bridge I must cross to get to the home of Master Gargamel?
?
!
?
AAAAAH
I just wanted directions! Don't be afraid!
Uh... beyond the bridge, smurf straight along the path to Gargamel's house!
SPLASH
1

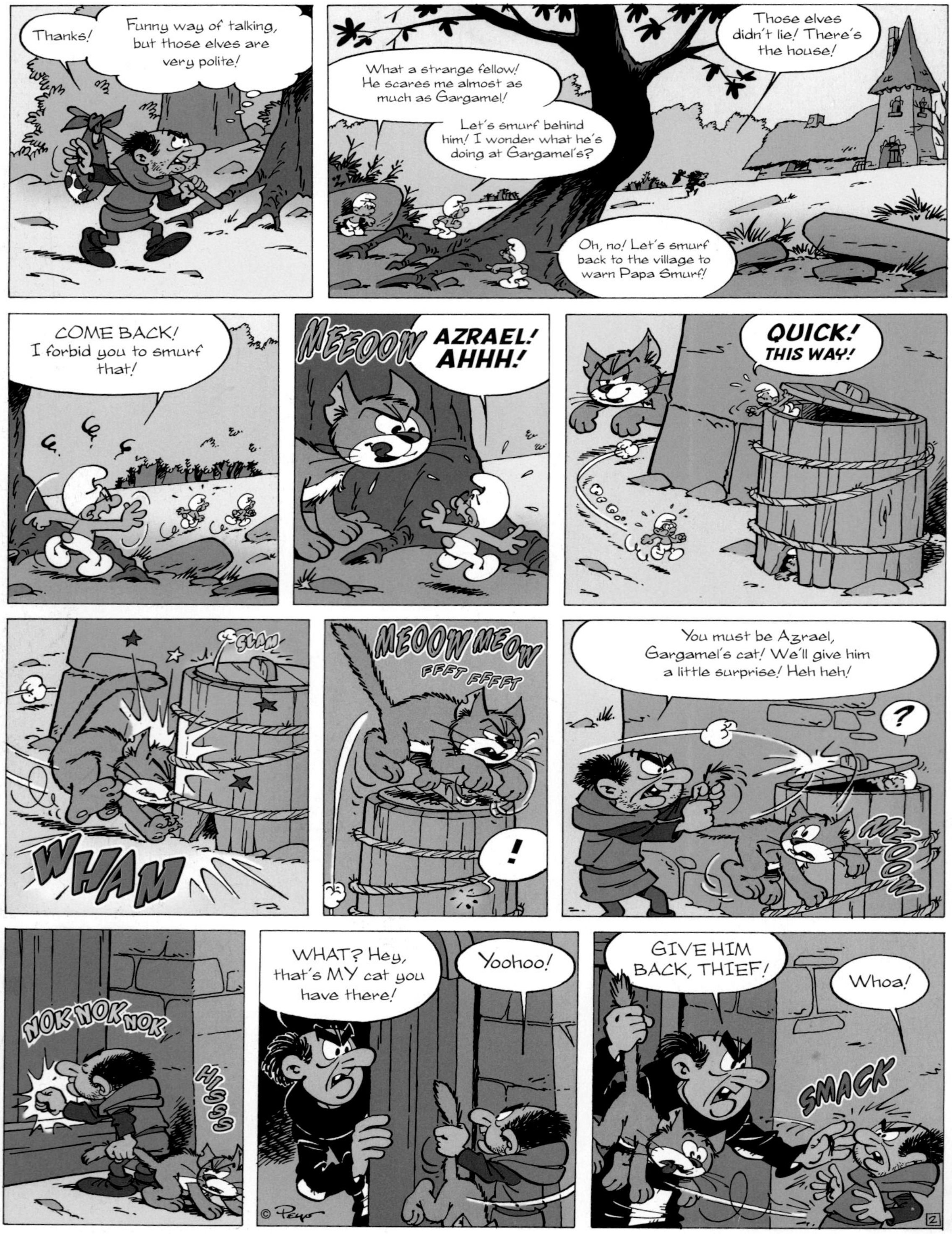

Thanks!
Funny way of talking, but those elves are very polite!
What a strange fellow! He scares me almost as much as Gargamel!
Let's smurf behind him! I wonder what he's doing at Gargamel's?
Those elves didn't lie! There's the house!
Oh, no! Let's smurf back to the village to warn Papa Smurf!
COME BACK! I forbid you to smurf that!
MEEOOW
AZRAEL! AHHH!
QUICK! THIS WAY!
SLAM
WHAM
MEOOW MEOW
FFFT FFFFT
!
You must be Azrael, Gargamel's cat! We'll give him a little surprise! Heh heh!
?
MEOOW
NOK NOK NOK
HISSS
WHAT? Hey, that's MY cat you have there!
Yoohoo!
© Peyo
GIVE HIM BACK, THIEF!
Whoa!
SMACK
2

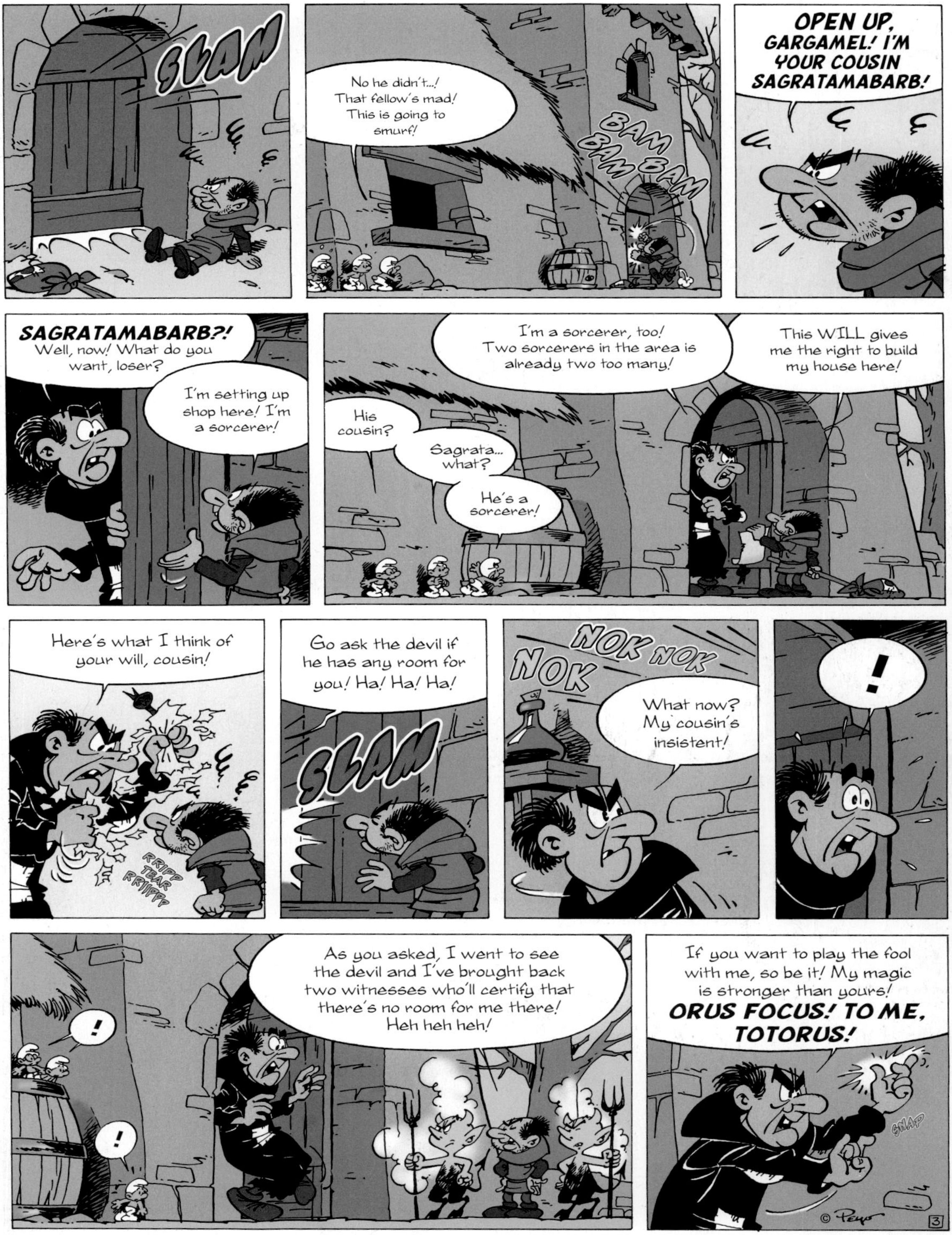
SLAM
No he didn't...! That fellow's mad! This is going to smurf!
BAM BAM BAM BAM
OPEN UP, GARGAMEL! I'M YOUR COUSIN SAGRATAMABARB!
SAGRATAMABARB?! Well, now! What do you want, loser?
I'm setting up shop here! I'm a sorcerer!
I'm a sorcerer, too! Two sorcerers in the area is already two too many!
This WILL gives me the right to build my house here!
His cousin?
Sagrata... what?
He's a sorcerer!
Here's what I think of your will, cousin!
RRIPP TEAR RRIPPP
Go ask the devil if he has any room for you! Ha! Ha! Ha!
SLAM
NOK NOK NOK
What now? My cousin's insistent!
!
!
!
As you asked, I went to see the devil and I've brought back two witnesses who'll certify that there's no room for me there! Heh heh heh!
If you want to play the fool with me, so be it! My magic is stronger than yours! ORUS FOCUS! TO ME, TOTORUS!
SNAP
© Peyo
3

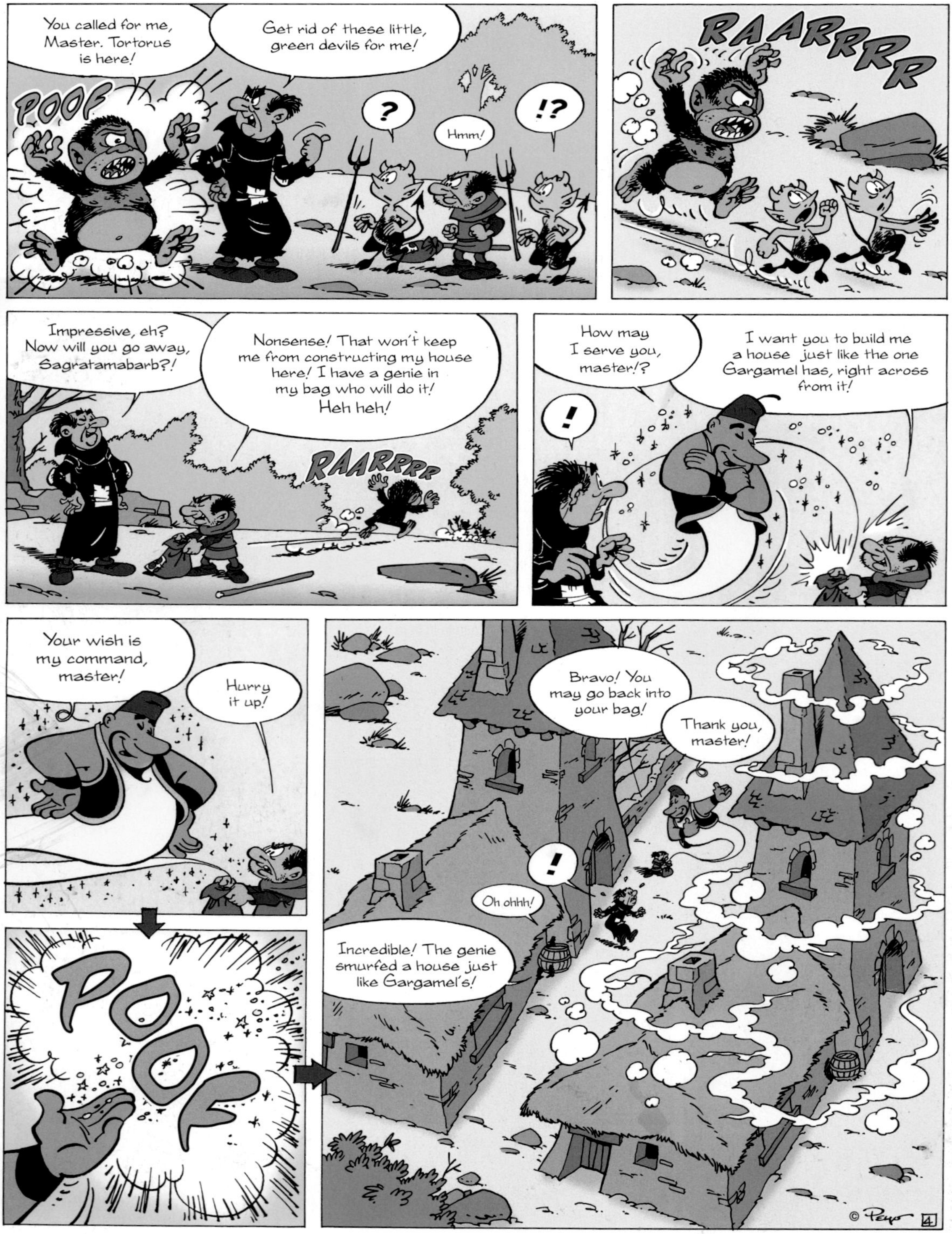

You called for me, Master. Tortorus is here!
Get rid of these little, green devils for me!
POOF
?
Hmm!
!?
RAARRRRR
Impressive, eh? Now will you go away, Sagratamabarb?!
Nonsense! That won't keep me from constructing my house here! I have a genie in my bag who will do it! Heh heh!
RAARRRRR
How may I serve you, master!?
I want you to build me a house just like the one Gargamel has, right across from it!
!
Your wish is my command, master!
Hurry it up!
POOF
Bravo! You may go back into your bag!
Thank you, master!
!
Oh ohhh!
Incredible! The genie smurfed a house just like Gargamel's!
© Peyo 4

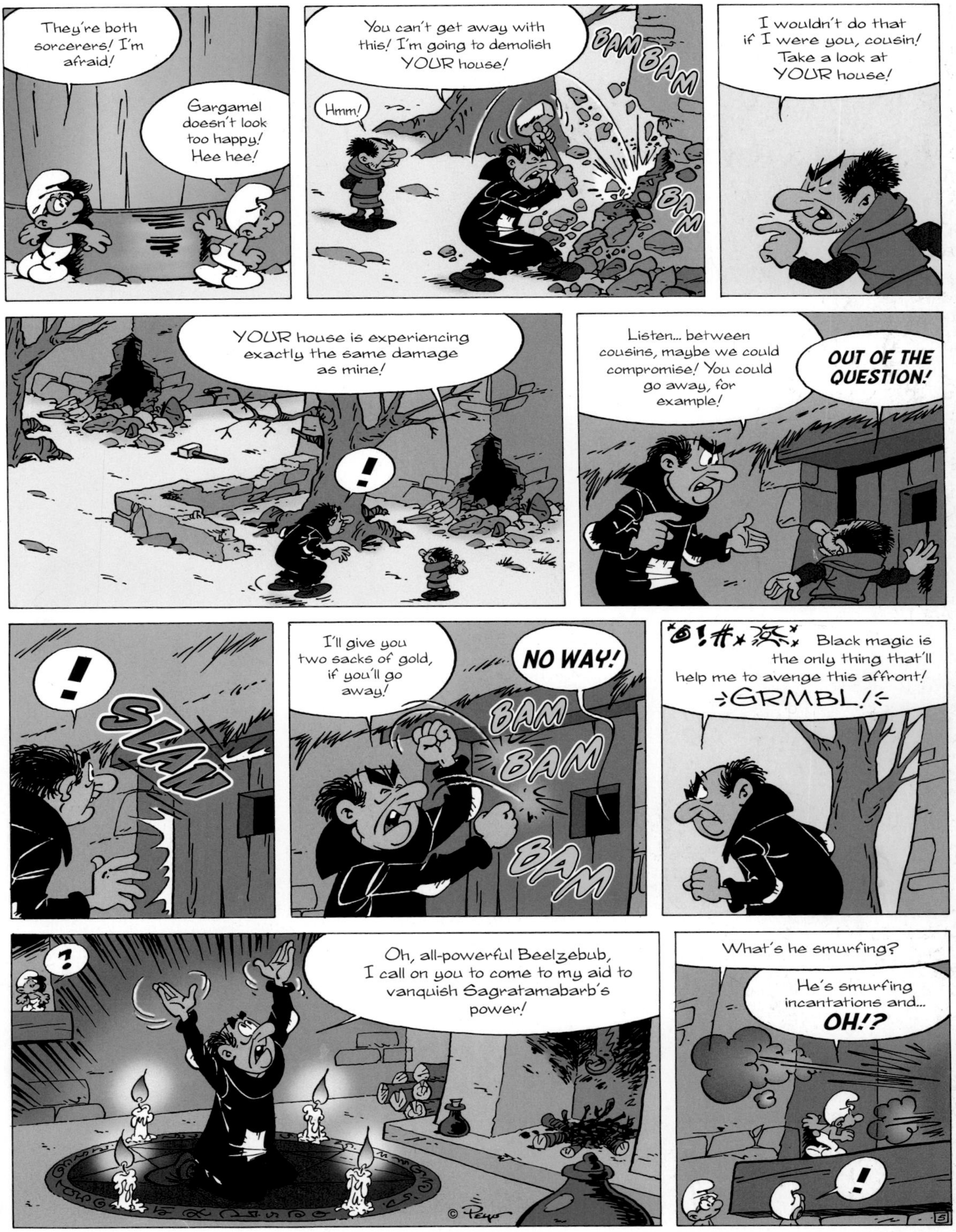
They're both sorcerers! I'm afraid!
Gargamel doesn't look too happy! Hee hee!
You can't get away with this! I'm going to demolish YOUR house!
Hmm!
BAM BAM
BAM
I wouldn't do that if I were you, cousin! Take a look at YOUR house!
YOUR house is experiencing exactly the same damage as mine!
!
Listen... between cousins, maybe we could compromise! You could go away, for example!
OUT OF THE QUESTION!
!
SLAM
I'll give you two sacks of gold, if you'll go away!
NO WAY!
BAM
BAM
BAM
Black magic is the only thing that'll help me to avenge this affront!
GRMBL!
?
Oh, all-powerful Beelzebub, I call on you to come to my aid to vanquish Sagratamabarb's power!
© Peyo
What's he smurfing?
He's smurfing incantations and... OH!?
!
5

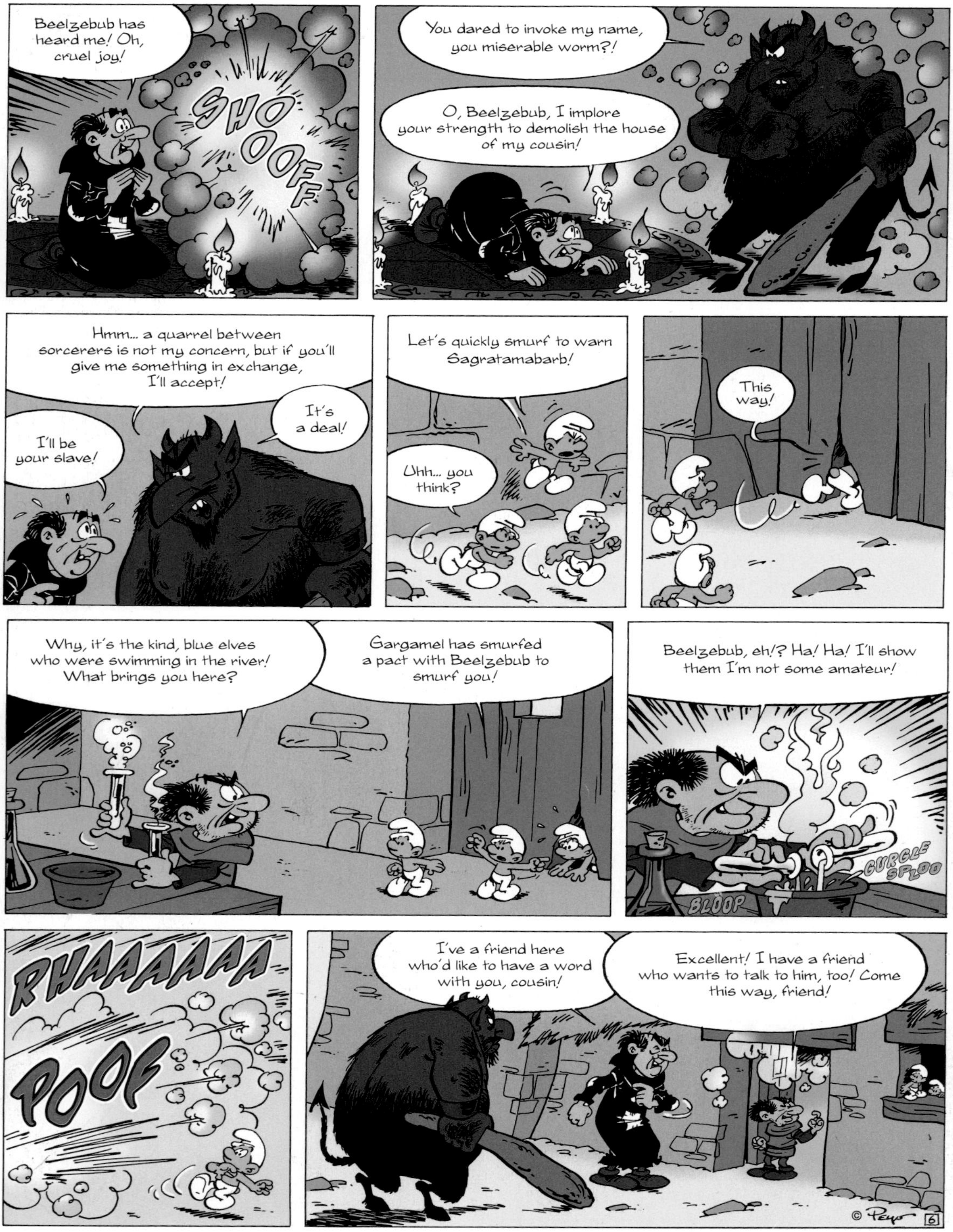

Beelzebub has heard me! Oh, cruel joy!
SHOOOFF
You dared to invoke my name, you miserable worm?!
O, Beelzebub, I implore your strength to demolish the house of my cousin!
Hmm... a quarrel between sorcerers is not my concern, but if you'll give me something in exchange, I'll accept!
I'll be your slave!
It's a deal!
Let's quickly smurf to warn Sagratamabarb!
Uhh... you think?
This way!
Why, it's the kind, blue elves who were swimming in the river! What brings you here?
Gargamel has smurfed a pact with Beelzebub to smurf you!
Beelzebub, eh!? Ha! Ha! I'll show them I'm not some amateur!
GURGLE
SPLOO
BLOOP
RHAAAAAA
POOF
I've a friend here who'd like to have a word with you, cousin!
Excellent! I have a friend who wants to talk to him, too! Come this way, friend!
© Peyo
6

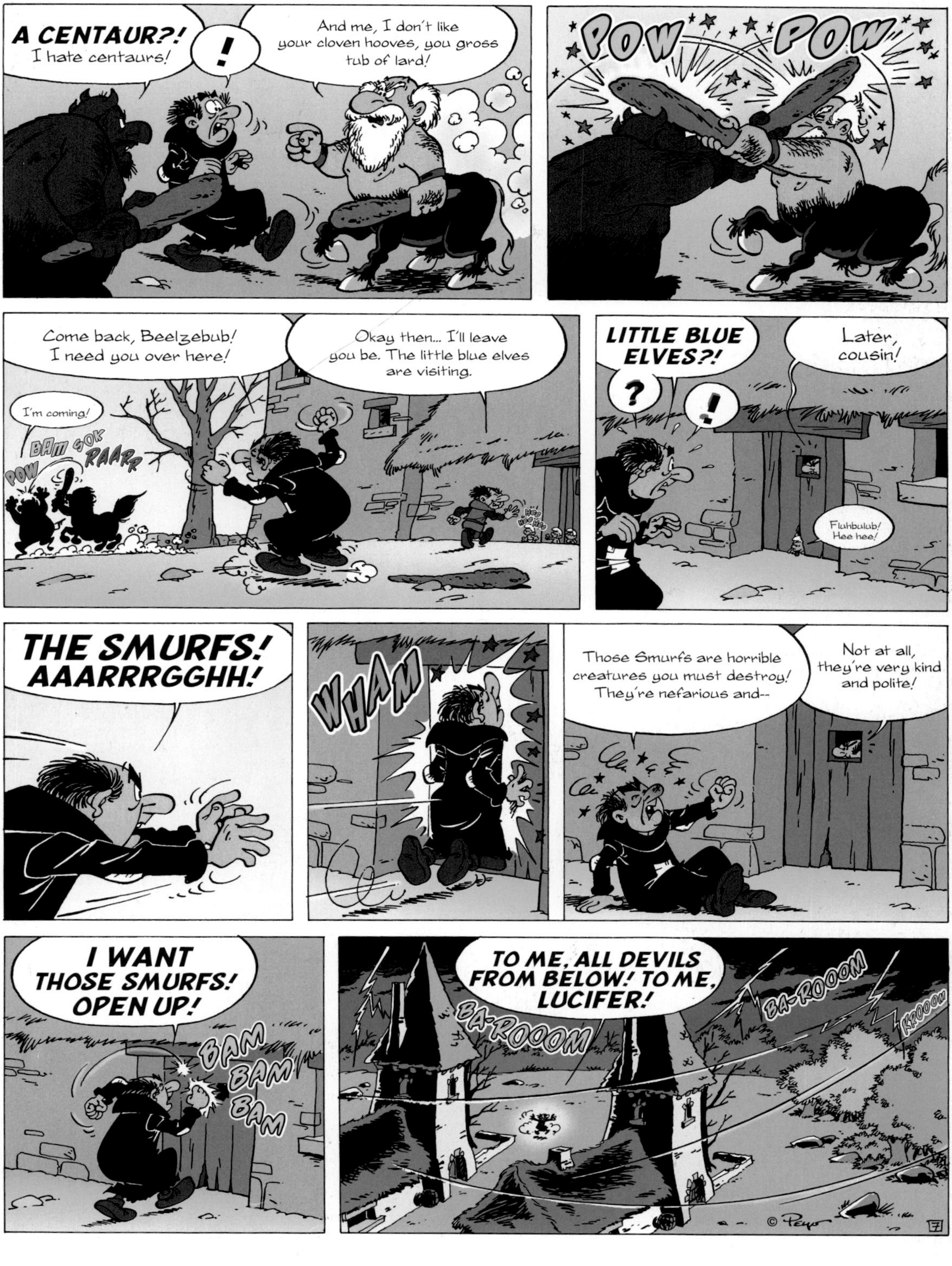
A CENTAUR?! I hate centaurs!
!
And me, I don't like your cloven hooves, you gross tub of lard!
POW
POW
Come back, Beelzebub! I need you over here!
I'm coming!
BAM SOK
RAARR
POW
Okay then... I'll leave you be. The little blue elves are visiting.
LITTLE BLUE ELVES?!
?
!
Later, cousin!
Fluhbulub! Hee hee!
THE SMURFS! AAAARRRGGHH!
WHAM
Those Smurfs are horrible creatures you must destroy! They're nefarious and--
Not at all, they're very kind and polite!
I WANT THOSE SMURFS! OPEN UP!
BAM
BAM
BAM
TO ME, ALL DEVILS FROM BELOW! TO ME, LUCIFER!
BA-ROOOM
BA-ROOOM
KROOOM
© Peyo
7

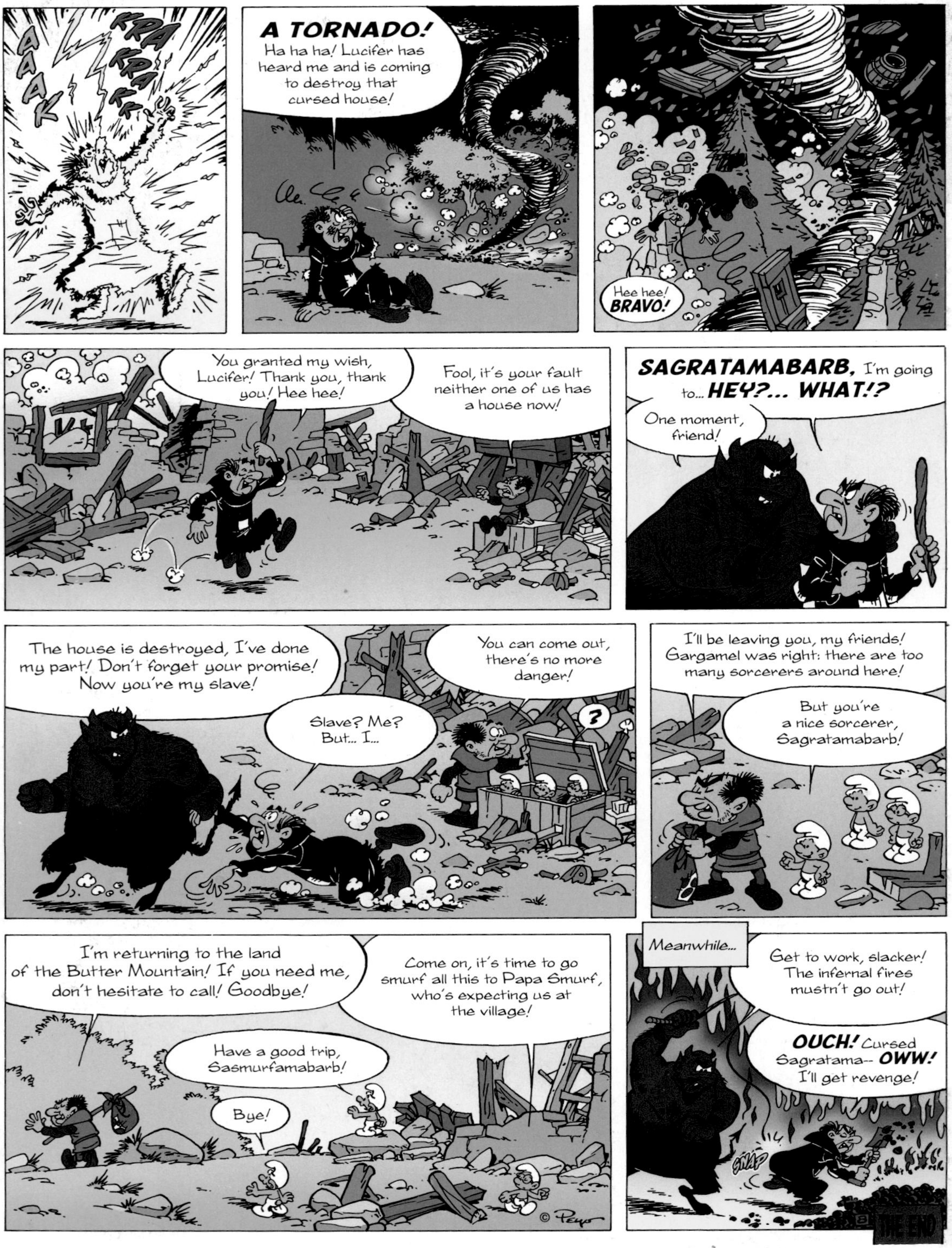
AAAAK
KRA KRA KRA KK
A TORNADO!
Ha ha ha! Lucifer has heard me and is coming to destroy that cursed house!
Hee hee! BRAVO!
You granted my wish, Lucifer! Thank you, thank you! Hee hee!
Fool, it's your fault neither one of us has a house now!
SAGRATAMABARB, I'm going to... HEY?... WHAT!?
One moment, friend!
The house is destroyed, I've done my part! Don't forget your promise! Now you're my slave!
Slave? Me? But... I...
You can come out, there's no more danger!
?
I'll be leaving you, my friends! Gargamel was right: there are too many sorcerers around here!
But you're a nice sorcerer, Sagratamabarb!
I'm returning to the land of the Butter Mountain! If you need me, don't hesitate to call! Goodbye!
Come on, it's time to go smurf all this to Papa Smurf, who's expecting us at the village!
Have a good trip, Sasmurfamabarb!
Bye!
© Peyo
Meanwhile...
Get to work, slacker! The infernal fires mustn't go out!
OUCH! Cursed Sagratama-- OWW! I'll get revenge!
SNAP
THE END

WATCH OUT FOR PAPERCUTZ

Welcome to the nutty, naughty and nearly-nefarious ninth SMURFS graphic novel by Peyo from Papercutz, the law-abiding, non-villainous publishers of great graphic novels for all ages. I'm Jim Salicrup, the Sagratamabarb-like Smurf-in-Chief, keeping an eye out for Gargamel. Ever since he appeared in the blockbuster SMURFS 3D movie, he's even more insufferable than ever! For example, he recently signed with a high-powered Hollywood talent agency. His agent called us and demanded that Gargamel's name be above THE SMURFS in the title on this graphic novel or Gargamel would walk! Well, as much as of a pain as ol' Gargy can be, and as much as the Smurfs would love him to take a long vacation, we have to admit he's the best SMURFS baddie ever, and after nearly 50 years of being the heavy in THE SMURFS, he may actually deserve, for the first time ever, his name first in the title!

And to commemorate such a dubious debut, we simply had to present Gargamel and Azrael's very first appearance in "The Smurfnapper." Nor could we exclude "A Smurf Not Like the Others," in which Gargamel utters the immortal line, "You rotten, little Smurfs, I—I—I love you!" We also included "The Smurfs and the Little Ghost," in which Gargamel has a small, yet pivotal role. We're sure Gargamel agrees with the old actor's axiom, "there are no small parts, only small Smurfs [1]." And what better tale to end our Gargamelathon than "Sagratamabarb"? Not because it features Gargamel's cousin, but because of where Gargamel finally ends up… at least for now!

But enough about that wicked wizard, it's time to talk about a much, much nicer person—our very own lettering Smurfette, Janice Chiang. We are all so lucky and thrilled to have her working on THE SMURFS graphic novels. Not only has she been one of the very best letterers in the comicbook field for years, having lettered every type of comic there is, including super-hero, teen humor, manga, translated graphic novels, and so many more, she's also one of the nicest people we know. Years ago, in addition to the hundreds of other comics she's lettered, she even lettered TRANSFORMERS and VISIONARIES comicbooks written by me! I knew back then that I was lucky to have someone such as her letter by hand my dialogue, captions, and sound effects.

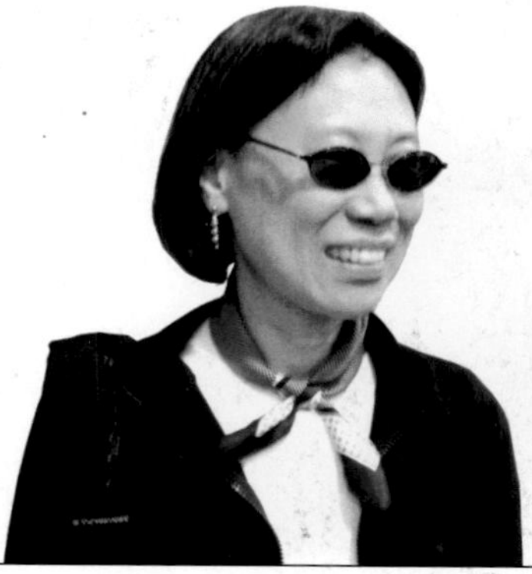

Lettering Smurfette Janice Chiang

But as good as she was then, true artist that she is, she has only honed her skills and continued to get better and better. In fact, she just recently won the 2011 Comics Buyer's Guide Fan Award for favorite letterer. While she is one of the few letterers around today who can letter by hand, she also mastered digital lettering, which is how most comics are lettered today.

Working on THE SMURFS, she is incredibly respectful of the original distinctive lettering style, yet has managed to incorporate a few twists of her own—from colorful sound effects to bold words with twisting angles rarely attempted. Like everyone else working on the Papercutz SMURFS graphic novels, she is devoted to making each panel on every page as Smurfy as possible. These comics, created by Peyo, are true comic art classics, and we are honored to present these comics to both longtime Smurf aficionados and those who've just stumbled onto our little blue buddies for the first time.

While Janice Chiang may now be known as the Lettering Smurfette, I'm happy to announce that in answer to countless requests, coming in January 2012 is THE SMURFS #10 "The Return of The Smurfette"! Smurf you later!

Jim

[1] According to Stanismurfski, legendary star of Smurf theater.

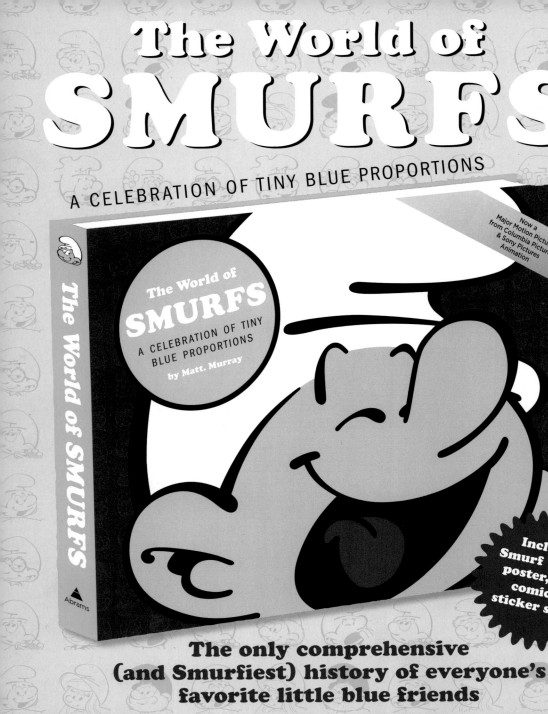

The World of SMURFS

by Peyo

A CELEBRATION OF TINY BLUE PROPORTIONS

Now a Major Motion Picture from Columbia Pictures & Sony Pictures Animation

Includes Smurf Village poster, mini comic, & sticker sheet!

The only comprehensive (and Smurfiest) history of everyone's favorite little blue friends

AVAILABLE NOW IN STORES AND ONLINE WHEREVER BOOKS ARE SOLD